Twisted Histories

Edited by Scott Harrison

Proudly published by Snowbooks

© 2013 Blood is Blood by Kaaron Warren

© 2013 Little Boxes by Gary McMahon

© 2013 Collapse by Susan Murray

© 2013 Blame The French by Stephen Gallagher

© 2013 The Silence Between the Sounds by Scott Harrison

© 2013 Containment by Justin Richards

© 2013 The Tides of Avalon by Jennifer Williams

© 2013 Flaming Sword by Richard Dinnick

© 2013 Covenants by Simon Bestwick

© 2013 The Second Coming by Wayne Simmons

© 2013 The Lips of Every Sleeper by Alison Littlewood

The authors named above assert the moral right to be identified as the author of their work. All rights reserved.

Snowbooks Ltd | www.snowbooks.com.

British Library Cataloguing in Publication Data. A catalogue record for this book is available from the British Library.

ISBN13 9781909679092

First published December 2013

CONTENTS

BLOOD IS BLOOD   (Gog & Magog)
    Kaaron Warren   5

LITTLE BOXES   (Pandora's Box)
    Gary McMahon   23

COLLAPSE   (John Barleycorn / the Green Man)
    Susan Murray   43

BLAME THE FRENCH   (Odysseus)
    Stephen Gallagher   71

THE SILENCE BETWEEN THE SOUNDS   (The Magi)
    Scott Harrison   87

CONTAINMENT   (Werewolves)
    Justin Richards   117

THE TIDES OF AVALON   (King Arthur / Mermaids)
    Jennifer Williams   155

FLAMING SWORD   (Adam & Eve)
    Richard Dinnick   175

COVENANTS   (The Ark of the Covenant)
    Simon Bestwick   199

THE SECOND COMING   (The Resurrection)
    Wayne Simmons   227

THE LIPS OF EVERY SLEEPER   (Dryads)
    Alison Littlewood   237

Blood is Blood
Kaaron Warren

If you stare hard enough and long enough at the statues of Gog and Magog, you may see them blink. If you do, you will know this story is true. Then you'll understand.

To know Gog and Magog, you need to hear of their mothers and aunts, the 33 daughters of the Emperor Diocletian. We know the oldest was Alba. The others? Perhaps Aelia, Laurentia and Marcellina.

"You will marry, every last one of you," the Emperor said. He (his advisors, moreso) chose all of their husbands, men with connections. No regard for love or attraction. Timing was crucial, as it always was, and the sisters were raced to their wedding night, little time for discussion or preparation.

The men couldn't tell these sisters apart as they walked together. A many-headed gorgon. They each had a honey pot for the buzzy buzzy bee men, the weak, the obsessed, the pathetic little men with their pizzles and their dreams of grandeur. Words spoken, wine swallowed, food devoured, the men all cheering, the women quiet.

Later: Alba, her blood humming in her ears, closed her eyes as her new, unloved husband fumbled with his clothing. She wondered if all women felt such disdain, or if there was something wrong with her. A single night with this weak man gave Alba a vision of a dull, child-ridden future full of nothing more than this, prodding every night, whining every day, and she knew she was due far, far more.

Is this enough to explain what occurred? Mythology says they were wicked, but that's not true. It was more about their blood and what ran through it.

Every murderer in history shares this blood, from the danaids, Daughters of Danus, King of Argos, who killed their cousin-husbands with hatpins, to Aileen Wournos. It's like a song humming in your ears. Alba heard it as she met with her sisters before dawn, all of them called by blood.

My blood hums as the blood of my ancestors did. It sings in a different way, I think. Sings us a song most people don't hear.

Is it true evil? Pure wickedness? Or a sense of self-preservation? Think of the daughters of Danus, who would have woken up dead themselves if they hadn't used their hatpins.

Because each of the 33 daughters of Diocletian took up knives and slit their husband's throats as they lay, sated, fat, sweaty, self-satisfied, dull, flaccid, grey. Then they sat together and drank the herb tea that would ensure tiny deaths, because not one wanted a child to those men.

Such fury. Such hatred and anger against these women who, after all, merely wanted a life that wouldn't kill them with boredom.

They were set adrift, not expected to live, on leaky boats with only the food and water they carried themselves.

Such powerful women. Survivors. Planners. Strong and smart. Of course they survived; how could it be otherwise?

Every natural born killer carries this blood, from the Greek God Ares, who killed Poseidon's son for attempting to rape Ares' daughter Alcippe, to the first serial killer who, history tells us, was Liu Pengli, who had people cowering in their homes for fear of him and his cronies. A hundred he killed and many more. And the women; Countess Elizabeth Bathory, Rosemary West, Belle Sorenson Gunness and the thousands who kill out of self-defence, who stay and stay until murder becomes the only option.

Blood is blood. And blood will show.

Are the statues blinking yet? You can see how the water drips from them when it rains. Reminds me of our dripping tap at home and he'd never fix it, would he? Because he loved that it drove me mad.

After 192 days the sisters landed on this island, the one we call Britain.

Alba named it after herself: Albion. "This is my island," she said. The others didn't mind. They were sisters, they were one. They were not concerned with Elsewhere. All they had is all they needed.

All they needed, at first, was the chance to explore, be adventurous. But blood will flow, and blood has needs. The sisters chose their own husbands this time and politics had nothing to do with it. Amongst men, there are always hidden fallen angels. These are the charmers. The ones who blind you, who exude powerful pheromones. There are always demons amongst men. I've got one at home.

Not all of the sisters shared a desire to find a demon. Some were happier in female company, some with no company at all.

"Your choice," Alba said, and words like that made it all worth it.

There are some who say 800 years passed, with the daughters of Diocletian and their descendants falling into incest, lust, murder and sub-humanity. Time is lost in history. Truly, only 16 years passed until Brutus arrived. Did cousins intermingle? Perhaps. But the sisters only loved their demons and the demons were not that kind of evil. They wanted babies, and these sisters were beautiful and broad and bright. They wanted very little. They were not reliant. So the men could hunt and fight. Wrestle for entertainment and the women liked that, more fucking, more babies.

The progeny were all giants. Gog, Magog, Og and others. They came out in the form of snakes, slithering out of their mother's vaginas all smooth and slick, then coiling on the ground, waiting as their bones merged, their flesh knitted, until they were giant babies the colour of the earth or of the inside of a cocoa bean, some the colour of a cloud ready to burst, some so white they looked like river stones.

* * * *

The 33 sisters and their families dispersed through the land, because no sister can live too close to another for long, and in this way the family grew. Some demons stayed, some left, some, perhaps, died. Gog and Magog both lost their fathers to the mountains; over they went and did not return. Og's father found fortune in another city, but that is a different story.

They were peaceful. The children grew strong and tall and they, like their fathers, enjoyed wrestling, both boys and girls. They found little competition outside their own family and, indeed, they needed to be careful, because those small ones broke so easily. Gog was the greatest of them, with Magog his only viable opponent. Og, it seems, was more concerned with his hair, and his face, and with the smoothness of his skin. He liked to direct, though, and to ensure each person sat in a place where he could see them. He liked to control; he would, and did, make a great ruler. He was not as tall as those two, but still would be tallest king to ever rule, with his bed lying at 3.6 metres.

Gog and Magog, not twins, not brothers, dear friends, and happy they were, carefree and never hungry.

Albion was a beautiful land, though it could be cold so the mothers stitched skins together, kindness itself, and there was the meat to eat after because no animal can live without its skin.

Remember that.

They kept to themselves for the most part, through caution and through irritation with the small and ordinary.

Still and even so, there were many who feared them for their size and their pure demonic fathers.

Alexander the Great built a wall to contain them. This is shown on maps. On the maps, also, Gog and Magog are depicted as monsters, waiting on the edge of the world to devour, as if they were cannibals. As if babies should be kept from them because they'd eat those tiny mites in a mouthful.

Oblivious, the children played, wrestled and ate, caring little for trouble or disquiet.

As the many cousins grew, their mothers began to look out for wives and husbands. The size didn't matter so much for the husbands, though surely bigger rather than smaller. The wives, though; It was finding a woman large enough to carry a baby to full term. This was a long time ago before the days when 24 weeks was considered viable. Would there be more snakes? Who could say.

My husband was no giant. And yet, how he made me feel. And how he made my daughter feel. I've got him at home, on the mantelpiece. "What's good enough for the mother of our guardians is good enough for me," I told myself. In court I'm smarter than that. In court we're all about the abuse and showing the evidence. We're not about blood will out. We're about saving my daughter from him and his mother too and who would argue that?

Watch their eyes. There. Did you see the blink?

One night the still-unmarried Gog, unable to sleep and wanting a snack, saw his mother hold a cooking blade to a man's throat. Not his father, he didn't think, although he lived in hope, but just as charming and handsome, Gog imagined. His mother would never choose someone dull and unattractive.

"What do you think, Gog? Should I slash his throat? I'm bored. He's not done me proud at all."

"Can't you just tell him to go?" Gog asked, chewing on a lamb bone he found, which was still meaty and full of marrow.

"He won't go. They never really go," she said, but the man wriggled out from under her fingers.

"Murderess!" he called once he was safely outside.

"Fool! Are you alive or dead?"

"Not me. Them. Those poor husbands you left behind."

She gave a shudder and Gog wondered if one day she would tell him why they came to Albion, 33 sisters in boats, arriving with nothing 'but the hair between our legs.' Aunt Laurentia always said.

They watched the man run away. "There are some who deserve to die. We have discussed this." Momentarily his mother looked vulnerable and sad, like the little girl he sometimes threw stones with, who had no mother and whose language he didn't speak.

He sat with his arm around her, chewing on his lamb bone as she fell asleep.

This is how a real man treats his mother. Not, like that husband of mine, bullying from the age of five and she, rather than teach him otherwise so that he would treat other women well, she allowed his behaviour. Encouraged it. I would blame all this on her but he is the master of his own destiny.

* * * *

The next morning they were woken before sunrise by the screaming of the sheep. It was an awful sound that Gog had only heard once before, when a pack of wolves got in and stole the lambs, ripped them up amongst the herd and carried the bleeding carcasses away.

This sounded worse.

"Gog! Get up!" It was Magog. "There are strangers. Armed."

Gog looked around for a weapon. They were in no way prepared; there was no violence in their lives, although travellers told stories of war, invasion, cruelty and early death. They wrestled hard, laid bruises, but there was always 'stop'.

His mother stood up, her blade glinting in her fist. "Let's go talk to these people, shall we? Perhaps they are here to trade."

She walked in front and Gog had no argument with that.

Light was pale with the dawn, the air so cold breath froze. They were often up at this hour, tending chores, especially when the crops were coming in or the sheep lambing.

The sounds of the town, though. Screaming, calling, gurgling. And the sheep.

"What is it?"

"We'll have to find out."

They lived on the outskirts of the community. Alba never wanted the largest house, or a fuss made of her.

Doors left open. A sandal, alone, in the path.

Blood.

Gog wanted to turn and run before anyone saw him, but his mother was resolute, marching on, and Magog by his side, breathing heavily.

Og was nowhere to be seen; later, they would learn he had been sent to safety. That he was not expected to protect or serve.

Gog wished they were taller and broader and that he could march in front. Three more daughters of Diocletian and their six children gathered to join Gog and Magog. A wail went up amongst them and Gog wondered; if we keep quiet, pretend we are dust, will we stay alive? But there was no chance of silence. No chance at all.

Foolish, perhaps, to head into danger, but none of them understood. Even the mothers, with their secret past, did not imagine what lay ahead. What sort of men had come to them.

There was a smell in the air of the public lavatory before the sand was cleaned and changed. And of iron. Gog covered his nose with his shirt, hoping to block it.

"Oh, Gog," his mother said as they reached the centre of town. The great stone stood there and had forever, as far as Gog knew. Back before the beginning of time.

"Cover your eyes, too," his mother said, her voice rising to a wail. "Block your eyes and your ears from this," and she turned and tried to cover his head with her scarf.

There were bodies piled against the stone. He couldn't tell how many, or who.

Blood ran like a river downhill towards the well.

Magog grabbed his arm. "What's happened? Did they eat something bad?" Such was his life that he couldn't imagine this as violence deliberately made.

"Nothing they ate."

Onto the road now came a great sheath of men, carrying bodies. There was Aunt Aelia, there Laurentia and Marcellina, tossed like meat before the stone.

"Run!" his mother whispered, and they all did that, scattering to the four corners, seeking a hideaway.

No good. There were more men surrounding the village, tearing it down, closing the circle. Amongst them was her mother's lover, very pleased with himself, "Trojan Horse," Alba whispered. "Trickery."

Rough men's hands grabbed them, but Gog wriggled out of a killer's grip and Magog did, too, both adept after wrestling each other all their lives.

Gog's mother took down two before they felled her, cracking her skull and those few left alive deflated as if the air and blood had drained out of them with her death.

Gog opened his mouth and roared. The sound shook stone and bone; he had no real awareness of his size or strength. Magog, who had not yet found his own mother, roared along with him. It took 12 men to bring them down.

Gog felt fingers around his throat from behind, twisted to see a man, standing far shorter than he did but thick with muscle. The hands tightened, twisted, and Gog thought the stars had come out. A deep voice said, "Hold."

This was Brutus. He would say, history would say, that he defeated great, vicious giants who were determined to tear his men limb from limb. Found with the bones of children in their hair, found dragging women by the feet, said to be inbred, murderous, insane. Successful perpetuators of genocide have the freedom to say such things and there are rare few left to doubt them.

"Name yourselves," Brutus said.

Gog and Magog did so, both standing with legs apart, arms wide, fists clenched. Gog thought he saw his mother crawling, but no. She didn't move.

"Ah!" this Brutus said. "You are Gog and Magog, the great undefeated wrestlers."

"We have defeated each other," Magog said, tipping his head forward.

"Then we shall see."

They wrestled, man after man after man. Wrestled until bloody, exhausted, then collapsed, barely conscious.

Each time they lost, Brutus had his men skin another woman.

No animal, remember, can live without its skin.

One Magog against 30? One Gog against 100? They lost.

All history leaves a trace on the present.

Those demons, the fathers; there is no report of where they were. Perhaps wreaking havoc elsewhere, causing wars, finding treasures, looking for surprises for their beautiful wives.

Perhaps they were surprised on the shore by Brutus and his men and drowned before they could mount a defence. Perhaps they were the ones who revealed the village and gave up sons, daughters, lovers.

Who can say?

The demons were demons, not men, and I wonder what a man would have done. Died for them, or run? Look at how easily Alba's weak husband had died, presenting his throat to her as if she was blessing him. Would he have presented his family in the same way?

Og, we know, ran free. He was as strong as the others but far smarter; he listened when he was told to run, and listened early enough. His name is written in history, not as a monster, but as a king.

* * * *

They were not the last of the cousins. Remember? The sisters who needed space were safe, hidden amongst the ordinary people, the children admired and feared for their height. Some cousins guarded borders. Some became cannibals. Some ruled cruelly, some ruled well, some died of loneliness and let their bodies turn to stone.

The blood passed on, and the way to know if you are bred from those sisters? Stand in front of Gog and Magog. They'll know. They'll blink.

If they blink you'll know.

Gog and Magog were dragged in chains to what we now call London, to this place, the Guild Hall. Evidence of the greatness of Brutus, there they stayed, fed on scraps, unsheltered, jeered at. Damaged.

They moved while they could, shook their chains like captured elephants or bears. They were not the giant men history says they were; mere children, they may have found their majority had they been allowed to live.

They were called the guardians. Like the euphemism for Good Friday, they were known to be enemies, but called supporters, as if the name would change their nature. But their nature was not vicious or cruel; they were young boys who had watched their families murdered. They called out for help and before long people came to them for help, advice and a word of kindness.

This they dispensed.

They also dispensed something else to the women of London, who came to them bare beneath their skirts, wanting something of what they had, these growing boys, these giants. Wanting, as any woman does, more than can be provided by any ordinary man.

By the time they died, they were perceived as true guardians; the giants who cared for London and all who lived in her.

As it was, they survived 22 months there, far beyond what Brutus himself would have achieved. Magog went first, sinking down, ignoring the pokes of fingers, the jabs of sticks, like a horse worn to the bone and unable to breathe any long.

Gog, riven with loneliness, willed himself to die as well.

Brutus ordered structures built around them, high standing coffins in the shape of giants. Gog and Mogog were put to rest inside them as if they still lived, and thus could cast their pleasant insinuations over the demanding people of London.

It was a man without a home who first understood, who first noticed the liquefied remains of Gog and Magog leaking from the bottom of the structures. He was the one who cleaned out the sculptures and gave the bones a burial in the Thames. Then he took over the position, living inside the statue, being fed. Dispensing kind words.

He became Gog, and soon Magog found a new inhabitant also. Today no one lives inside, but there's no doubt the souls of those giants are present.

See? Did you see that blink?

That is why I killed him.

It's in my blood.

Little Boxes
Gary McMahon

Jack didn't want to go to school that morning. He didn't want to go to school any morning. But Jack was a good boy so when his alarm went off he slid out of bed and padded out of the room, along the hall, to the bathroom. He brushed his teeth, showered, used the toilet, and then went back to his room to get dressed.

He put on his school uniform and looked at himself in the mirror. There was nothing remarkable about him; he was a normal eleven year-old schoolboy with messy hair and pale skin and a family that hated him.

When he went back out into the hall he glanced at his mum's room. Her door was slightly open. He could see the edge of the bed and Uncle Pete's feet sticking out of the covers. Jack sighed and went downstairs.

In the kitchen, he made himself two slices of toast, slathered them with strawberry jam, and poured a glass of milk. He watched Adventure Time while he ate. He liked that show; it was his favourite. It made him smile. Not many things did that, so this was to be treasured.

When he'd finished his breakfast he took the dirty dishes through into the kitchen, loaded them into the dishwasher, along with last night's dishes, and then set the machine running. He stared at the dishwasher door, wishing that it was this easy to clean away the dirt from a life. After a few minutes he turned away, grabbed his jacket off the back of a kitchen chair, and headed for the back door.

He opened the door with his key and stepped outside. On the small concrete patio, positioned below the doorstep, was a small cardboard box. Jack glanced up and then down the narrow private lane. The allotments were at the top; the main road, with the park opposite, was at the bottom. A bus trawled past the mouth of the lane. A woman pushing a pram walked by without looking in his direction.

Jack bent over and picked up the box. It was very light; much lighter than he expected; as light as a feather. He carried it back inside and set it down on the kitchen table. There was an address label stuck to the side:

Jack Finch
6 Parkview Lane
Shedley
West Yorkshire

That was all. No return address. No other identifying mark. Jack wasn't expecting a package. He hadn't ordered anything from Amazon and it wasn't his birthday for another two months. Who would send him something? He wracked his brain, trying to identify a possible source, but nothing came.

He ran a hand over the cardboard. It felt smooth and he detected a slight chill. He checked his watch and saw that if he didn't leave soon he was going to be late for school. Idly, he picked at the lid of the box with his fingers, but the flaps didn't budge. They must be glued down.

Shrugging, Jack left the house and started on his twenty-minute walk to school. He would take a look at the box later, when he had more time. The way things were lately, it wouldn't be anything. Or perhaps it was a box full of dog shit sent to him by Terry Nicks, the boy who'd been bullying him for over a year. He wouldn't put it past the prick. It was exactly the type of thing he'd find funny.

As he walked to school, Jack's mind drifted back to the box. He wished he'd stayed behind to open it, but if his mum or Uncle Pete had found him hanging back from school, he might have received another slap. It was happening a lot lately, since Uncle Pete had moved in with them. The man was always busy with his hands –

running them all over Mum, sticking them in Jack's spare change jar, or slapping them both around. Mum didn't seem to mind too much; she said it was better than being alone. Things had been different before Jack's dad had been killed in Afghanistan. They'd been happy, just the three of them: a happy little family, with no slapping, no money-stealing and no nameless fears stalking them around the house like ghosts.

Jack wished that he could turn back time to put things right. He wished that his dad would appear at the door one day, still alive, and it had all been a terrible mistake. He wished that he could change things.

He walked through the school gate, instinctively looking out for Terry Nicks and his gang of hangers-on. When he walked across the playground, nodding at friendly faces and not making direct eye contact with neutral or unfriendly ones, he finally saw his own little group huddled by the gym wall.

"Jack!" Lisa waved as he approached, her small, freckled face breaking out into a grin, and then changing back to a frown.

"Hi, guys." Jack shucked off his rucksack and set it down on the ground against the wall.

"Did you get one?" asked Bill, without preamble, his pudgy face displaying a frightened expression.

"What are you on about?"

"In the post," said Scott, his skinny, nervy frame never still for a moment. "This morning. Did you get a box?"

Jack stared at his three friends. "How did you know I got something in the post?"

"An educated guess," said Lisa, moving towards him, her shoulder brushing his.

"We all got one," said Bill. "So we thought you probably did, too."

"Okay..." Jack sat down on the ground, leaning his back against the wall. "What is all this? Is it a joke?"

"We don't know," said Scott, dropping down into a squat beside him. "Did you try to open your box?"

Jack shook his head. "Didn't have time. I was running late."

"They won't open." Bill kicked the wall with the toe of his shoe. "They're stuck."

Jack smiled, but he felt uncomfortable. "What do you mean, they won't open?" He remembered how the cardboard flaps had not budged.

"I dunno..." Bill blew air though his mouth, causing his chubby cheeks to inflate like twin balloons. "We all tried, but we couldn't get the cardboard to tear, or even pierce it with a knife."

"I tried that," said Scott. "It was like trying to stab a sheet of metal."

Jack stood up and took a step away from the wall. "This is stupid. I'm not getting this, not any of it."

His three friends said nothing. They just stared at him, as if they expected him to solve the mystery.

At break time they were due to meet again, in their usual place against the gym wall, but Jack was sidetracked by Terry Nicks chasing him through the corridors towards the main hall. Jack hid in a storage cupboard and wondered what was going on. His friends weren't the type to make practical jokes and they would never lie to him. They were his best mates; the four of them were the school outcasts, the nerds and the geeks and the loners. They were a club. They were tight.

He hid in the storage cupboard until break time was over, and then went to class. The afternoon passed slowly and he kept thinking about the box he'd left on the kitchen table. He couldn't wait to get home and try to open it.

He didn't see his friends that afternoon, but as he walked home – taking the long way, in case Terry Nicks was hanging around for afters – he received a text from Lisa on his mobile phone. He felt his heart flutter, just like always, when he opened the text.

meet at mine 2nite? Mum's out at bingo. dad on niteshft. 8pm? bring the box.

He replied that he'd be there and continued on his way.

When he arrived home his mum and Uncle Pete were upstairs, shouting. There were empty beer bottles on the kitchen draining board and the curtains looked like they'd been closed all day.

The box was still on the kitchen table. They'd either not noticed it or chosen to leave it alone. Sometimes they opened his post. If there was anything valuable in there – like a CD or a DVD he'd sent for – they often sold it down the pub.

Jack grabbed the box and took it upstairs. His mum's bedroom door slammed shut as he walked past and he heard the familiar sound of a slap being administered. He went into his room and locked the door. He sat on his bed and looked at his monster posters, the books and magazines on his shelves and the DVDs in his collection. Occasionally stuff went missing. His mum and Uncle Pete denied all knowledge, but he knew that they stole his things. He wasn't bothered, not really. If he kicked up too much of a fuss he'd get a slap and he could do without the pain.

His friends had been right about the box. He tried to slide his fingers under the cardboard flaps at the top and peel them down, but they wouldn't move. It seemed impossible, but they were sealed, with no gaps. When he took out his penknife, and tried to cut one side of the box, he had no success. There were no joins, either; the box was constructed out of a single sheet of material, folded carefully.

"This is weird," he said. Then he was distracted by the sound of his mum and Uncle Pete making the headboard bang against the wall. When his mum's moaning became too loud to bear, he put in his headphones and listened to some music. Loud music. The loudest he could find on his play lists.

* * * *

He left the house at 7:45. Lisa lived a few streets away and it wouldn't take him long to get there. He'd been lucky enough not to run into his mum and Uncle Pete as he made a sandwich in the kitchen, and then ate it watching TV in the front room. They must be too drunk to bother with coming downstairs. They did that sometimes: stayed on the second floor all day, only coming down at night to listen to music, shout some more at each other, and order a takeaway long after midnight.

Jack wondered if everyone's life was like this – or was it just him? What had he ever done to deserve this? He was a good boy; he stuck in at school, stayed out of trouble... but for some reason his life had turned to shit.

He missed his dad. He missed him so much that he knew if he started crying he would never, ever stop. So he never cried. He kept it all locked down inside, with a lid on. He was never going to let that particular monster out of that particular box.

The others were already there when he arrived at Lisa's place. She kissed him on the cheek as she let him in. He felt his cheeks flush.

"I'm glad you came," she said. She was wearing a pair of dark denim jeans and a T-shirt with a monkey's face on the front. Her feet were bare. She was wearing her hair down and it hung across her shoulders in silken splendour.

"Me, too," he said, as he followed her upstairs to her room. He tried not to look at her bottom. But these days he found it hard not to look at Lisa in that way. She was a pretty girl. Whenever she smiled at him, he felt hot and anxious. He didn't know if Bill and Scott felt the same way; they'd never discussed it. It was a topic they steered clear of.

"Hi," said Bill without looking up as they entered the room.

Scott, sitting on the bed, raised a hand in greeting.

There were three cardboard boxes on the floor, next to Bill. Jack walked over and added his own box to the group.

"Okay," he said. "What's happening?"

Bill stood and faced the room. "I have a theory."

"Here we go..." said Lisa. Scott giggled from the bed. Jack smiled.

"No, seriously. Listen. You've heard of Pandora's Box, right? Where all the evils in the world were held, until that silly bint opened it?"

"Oi," said Lisa. "Less of the sexism, please!"

Scott giggled again, and Jack realised that he was nervous.

"I think what we have here," said Bill, approaching the boxes "is the same thing. But instead of one box, we have four."

"That's a bit of a stretch," said Jack. "I mean, what made you even think that?"

Bill shrugged. "I don't see you lot coming up with any ideas."

"I think they're from aliens," said Scott, shifting on the bed. "They're gifts..." he glanced up, at the ceiling. "Gifts from above. I saw a film once, where aliens sent down a big black slab to help humans evolve…"

"You boys don't half talk a lot of crap," said Lisa. She sat down facing the boxes. "Hey, look at this…they've changed."

Scott slid off the end of the bed. Bill flopped down heavily opposite Lisa. Jack walked over and crouched, staring at the boxes.

"You're right," said Bill.

The boxes had changed colour. Now, instead of the dull manila colour of normal cardboard boxes, they'd turned white, as white as bleached bone. And the flaps at the top of each box had opened, puckering out like strange petals.

"Whoa…" Bill leaned forward. "This is getting really weird now."

"Don't touch them," said Jack.

"Why not? Maybe we've been chosen…what if this really is some kind of gift, like Scott said?" Lisa was reaching out, reaching forward, towards the boxes. "From God, or something?"

"It just…doesn't feel right." Jack knew how lame he sounded, but something was nagging away at him. Why would anyone choose them to take responsibility for something like this? They were the losers, the mopers,

33

the kids who nobody else wanted to be around because they didn't fit in. What could they possibly have to offer?

Before he could object further, Lisa had pushed aside the cardboard flaps on the nearest box and reached inside. She pulled out a mask. It was nothing special, just a dumb plastic novelty mask like the kind you could get from any joke shop. It was Frankenstein's Monster, all green-skinned and with crude stitching and black plastic bolts in its neck.

"What the hell?" Bill lifted out of his box a Dracula mask. White face. Black hair. Bloody fangs.

Scott's mask was a zombie. It had only one eye and its flesh was falling off, showing glimpses of the bone beneath.

"Your turn," said Lisa. Her eyes were wide. She looked…beautiful.

Jack reached inside the last box and pulled out the mask. His mask. It was a werewolf.

"What are we meant to do now?" Bill's voice was soft, almost a whisper.

"We put them on," said Lisa.

So they did.

* * * *

When he got home later that night, Jack had no memory of what they'd done after putting on the masks. It was as if he'd suffered some kind of amnesia; his mind was a blank during the period between putting on the mask and leaving Lisa's house. He only recalled standing in the street and waving at his friends, bathed in sodium streetlight. The zombie, the Monster, and Dracula, all waving slowly, like weird characters from some kind of dream.

He sat in the kitchen with the lights turned out, staring through the eyeholes of the mask at the shapes of the cooker, the fridge, the sink. Each of the humdrum domestic objects looked different…but, no, it wasn't them that were different. It was him. It was Jack who had changed.

His mouth tasted coppery, like old pennies. His belly was full, as if he'd just eaten.

He reached up and caressed the plastic contours of the mask. Only it didn't feel like plastic anymore. He stroked the soft, warm pelt on his cheeks, probed at the fangs and incisors in his mouth, and prodded the thick, cold strings of saliva that hung from his lips.

He could quite easily take off the mask if he wanted to, but he didn't want to. He wanted to keep it on, forever.

He heard the stairs creak as someone came down. A light came on in the stairwell. He sniffed the air. It was Uncle Pete. Jack could smell the beer and the sex and the apathy coming off him in waves. He listened as the footsteps came down the stairs, across the floor, and stopped just inside the kitchen doorway.

"What the fuck are you doing sitting there in the dark?" His voice was slurred. He stumbled as he walked into the kitchen, slamming into the fridge with his shoulder. "Ouch," he said. "Bastard."

He opened the fridge, looked inside, raked around for a while, and then slammed the door shut. Then he walked over to the sink and filled a glass with cold water. His throat made a rapid glug-glug noise as he drank.

"Well?" He approached the table, pulled out a chair, and sat down opposite Jack. His bulk blocked out most of the workbench behind him.

"What the fuck?" He started laughing. "Why are you wearing that stupid mask? It ain't Halloween." He slammed both of his fists down on the wooden tabletop, clenched and unclenched his fingers. "Speak to me, boy."

Jack remained silent. He sat there with his hands in his lap, feeling the fingernails as they grew into long, sharp, lethal claws. It was an incredible sensation. He wished that it would never stop.

"Do you want this?" Uncle Pete raise his hand, opened it to display the sweaty palm. "I'll give it to you. You know I will. Free of charge." His large face shone, catching the light from the stairs. Sweat hung in droplets from his wrinkled forehead. His faded tattoos looked like dead veins seen through a thin layer of flesh. For the first time, Jack understood how weak this man really was.

"Don't even think about it." Jack's voice sounded to him like an animal growl. He wasn't sure if Uncle Pete had understood him, so he spoke again, slowly, just to clarify. "You touch me again, and you're dead."

Jack had never spoken so honestly in his life. His words cut through the untruths of the world and pierced the skin of a reality that was so much older, so much purer, than the one inhabited by his mum and Uncle Pete. It was like a glimpse of a better place, one without the constraints imposed upon him by those who were meant to care but didn't, never had, never would.

Uncle Pete smiled. His eyes were empty. His teeth were yellow. He moved quickly for a man of his age, but nowhere near quickly enough. Compared to Jack, his flesh was slow and heavy; he was a monster from the new world not the old.

Jack reached across the table with lightning speed. He swung his arm, the clawed hand taking a chunk out of

Uncle Pete's throat and tearing away the bottom half of his face, exposing the bone of his chin. Uncle Pete slumped. His hand dropped back to the table, twitching. Blood pumped from the wound; it smelled of alcohol. Jack lapped it up, anyway, or most of it. Something inside him began to grow.

Jack stood and walked away from the table, and then on impulse he dropped to all fours and padded up the stairs. It felt much better walking this way, more comfortable. Like it was how he was meant to move but just hadn't realised.

He headed straight for his mum's room. She was sleeping. One of her arms was draped over the edge of the bed; her opposite leg was uncovered. Her skin was soft and white, like the material of the boxes once they had changed. Tiny hairs stood up to attention along her shin. He could see the veins under the surface of her skin and hear the blood pumping through them. She smelled so much better than Uncle Pete, even if her body odour was stale.

Her feet were tiny. Her toes looked so damned tasty.

Jack stood on his rear legs and towered over the bed. He felt tall and strong, imbued with a power that he had never known he possessed. The mattress creaked as he pressed his legs against it. He bent down and kissed his mum on the side of the face, and as she smiled in her sleep he bit down deeply, wrenching away part of her jawbone along with the meat in his massive jaws.

He fed for a little while. Then he went back downstairs. He played with Uncle Pete's remains for a short time, tugging them around the kitchen, leaving red splashes and smears all over the linoleum floor. Soon he got bored of the game, so he went to the front door and opened it.

Outside, the moon shone down on the street like a theatre spotlight. The streetlights had gone out, but he didn't need them to see by – not with his new/old eyes: the eyes of the mask. Somehow they made it so he could see clearly in the dark, with the nocturnal vision of a nighttime predator.

All of his friends were out there waiting for him, and they were not alone. Hundreds of kids wearing masks were standing in the street, silently watching and waiting for him to join them. The doors of most of the houses stood open. A lot of the windows were broken.

Even Terry Nicks was there, wearing a mask that looked like a skull. His gang of bullies stood beside him, wearing their own masks. They nodded at Jack. He nodded back, reaching some kind of unspoken agreement. Old hatreds were now forgotten. There was other business at hand.

When Jack stood to his full height and howled at the moon, they all dropped to their knees, raising their heads and staring up at the cool, dark night sky. They clasped their hands together, as if they were praying, and rocked together, back and forth, back and forth, in silent mirth.

Some of them were wearing the masks of fictional creatures – similar to the ones worn by him and his friends. But others wore the masks of human monsters: serial killers, murderous despots and politicians, or the faces of everyday people who killed small children and buried their bodies on lonely moors. Where the masks had come from no longer mattered, just the simple fact that they were here, and they were being worn. Whatever was stirring inside him gave one final kick, and then it filled him, making him smile with his big, bad werewolf teeth.

Jack had never felt so alive, or so certain of his purpose.

Like a new king, he surveyed the eager crowd before him. These kids – these damaged vessels of innocence – now looked out from inside their bodies through the eyes of the monstrous, and what they saw out there in the world were the adults who no longer deserved to care for them: the real monsters, the ones that needed to be vanquished.

Because each child had received an identical box, and inside that box was not in fact every evil in the world, as Bill had theorised…no; inside every one of those boxes had been a mask, and something else besides. At the bottom of each box, waiting to be held aloft like a spear or a standard, there had been a little thing called hope.

Jack once more dropped to all fours and headed along the street, moving towards the rest of the streets that made up the town, and the ones that led to the wider world of rot and ruin beyond. He felt no fear, only hunger. He felt like he'd grown up and become something new.

Jack had left behind his childhood in the house that he was turning his back on, soaked in the blood of his irresponsible guardians.

He didn't miss his old life.

There was no turning back.

Now it was time to rouse his army and go to war.

Collapse
Susan Murray

The window faces west. It's peaceful here, that used to be all that mattered to me. The barley field stretches away down to the tree-lined river. The road skirts the edge of the open field. I can see anyone coming long before they can see me. And when they come, they'll come from the west.

* * * *

It happened so quickly. One minute we were crossing the car park from the bus stop, laughing over some stupid joke. The next there was a squeal of brakes, a thud, a pained exhalation, and Maddy vanished underneath the CEO's 4x4, the cardboard cup containing her latte bursting on the ground. If I hadn't stepped in a puddle, paused to brush a splash from my stockings …

Harland clambered from the driver's seat. 'She just stepped out in front of me. There was nothing I could do.'

I ignored him, dropping to my knees on the wet ground next to Maddy. It was already too late. Blood and… other things spilled from her broken head. I had to turn away, but I stayed with her, it seemed the right thing to do. A few yards away the remains of her latte seeped into the tarmac. Most of it had gone by the time the paramedics arrived.

After that was a muddle of ambulances, police, questions, statements. I'd been parked in a corner behind one of Grandidge's ridiculous bamboo plants and subjected to a succession of foul mugs of sugary tea and good intentions. Executives in suits milled about the small conference room with the admin staff. Everyone was being infuriatingly kind to me and speaking in hushed tones. Everyone except Harland; he was still telling anyone who'd listen how there'd been nothing he could do. It was too much. No one pointed out he'd been speeding into the car park through the exit. Somehow he was managing to rewrite himself as victim while I sat there in silence. If I let him go unchallenged, what did that make me?

It was one of those uncomfortable thoughts that took hold and niggled. Or maybe it was the cumulative effect of all that sugary tea. Either way, I began my rebellion on a small scale by tipping the latest mugful into the planter. I jumped to my feet, not sure what I was going to say, but determined to say something. And one of the suits stepped in front of me, blocking Harland from sight.

'What did that poor plant ever do to you? If you're ready to go I'll drive you home.' Grandidge scooped up my handbag from the floor and steered me from the room. He nodded to Yvonne on reception. 'Sophie here needs to recover from the shock at home. Call the agency to cover for the next couple of days. And let the research centre know I'll be arriving later than planned.'

He led me out through the front door then round to the car park at the rear of the building. The area surrounding the collision was taped off. He'd deliberately avoided walking past it, I realised.

'You and Maddy were good friends, weren't you?'

'Yes.' My voice didn't wobble, but it was a close thing. Maddy, with her startling hair and body piercings, had been the one generous enough to befriend the wide-eyed country girl and ease her into city ways. I couldn't break, not here. Not yet.

Grandidge said something appropriate, but I had no idea what. He didn't seem to need a reply, which was just as well: at that point I was running on empty.

His company car was small by anyone's standards, but he'd insisted on the most economical model: he wasn't the run-of the mill suit. The moment he'd folded his six foot two frame into the driver's seat he tugged his tie loose, like a schoolboy escaping the school gates. And he had the same restless air of suppressed energy; in the close confines of the car it was unsettling.

'Where's home?'

I told him. 'But you don't need to do this.' I glanced at my watch. 'There'll be a bus in ten minutes.'

'It's no problem; I'm going out to the research centre anyway.' He started the engine and nudged the car into gear. 'It's a long way to commute every day.'

'It's not too bad. Rent's much cheaper there.'

'The company could be more generous with their staff.'

So that was his game: catch me off guard while I was overwrought. 'There are worse places to work.'

'I heard you had some fairly colourful views on company policy.'

'And I heard you talk to plants. You can't believe everything you hear at the water cooler.'

'But I do talk to plants.' He stopped the car at the exit barrier and grinned at me. 'You're too young to be so cynical.'

Well, excuse me for being off-form. I glared out of the window: so many people going about their lives, enjoying the spring sunlight, unaffected by the tragedy a few hundred yards away.

'She'll have justice.' He spoke with a quiet certainty. 'I'll see to it.'

'It was an accident. A needless waste, but only an accident.'

He pulled up at a set of traffic lights, acknowledging my words with a sideways tilt of his head that suggested he disagreed. He didn't speak for a while as he negotiated the one-way system. I'd sooner have completed the journey in silence but Grandidge had other ideas. 'Did you and Maddy talk much about her work?'

'A bit.' She'd bitched about her boss, and about having to spend day after day stooped over racks of test tubes. 'I collate the research reports so there wasn't much need, I was pretty much in the loop.'

'How about her most recent project?'

'The bee research? Into colony collapse?'

Grandidge nodded, glancing in the rear view mirror before returning his eyes to the road ahead.

'The preliminary report went out last week.' It had been pretty damning for one of the company products.

'Anyone else work on it?' His question was casual enough; too casual.

'No.' He had intensely green eyes. I hadn't noticed before, but he was normally breezing past on his way elsewhere. It occurred to me then that John Grandidge did everything for a reason. 'Rita must have passed that report to you by now?'

'No, I can't say she has.' He frowned as he glanced again in the rear view mirror. 'Of course, if it was routine there'd be no need to call it to my attention.'

'Well, no; but the results were pretty controversial.'

'Interesting. That was the impression Maddy gave me when I discussed the work with her.' He turned the car into my street and eased it into a parking space between the pollarded trees. 'Yet Rita told me there was nothing of consequence in the findings.'

'Are you suggesting Maddy and I cooked up a load of lies between us?'

'To discredit Rita? Of course not.' A car cruised past outside, catching his attention for a moment. 'You can be sure that's what she and Harland will say.'

So he knew about their affair. But why tell me? He'd done a fine job of feeding my paranoia. Maddy's research had indicated the company's biggest seller was damaging wildlife; a few days after handing in the report her boss's boyfriend had run her down in the company car park.

I suppressed a shiver.

'Are you all right?' Grandidge switched off the engine.

'Uh…' I gaped at him.

'Maybe, like me, you're not a great believer in coincidence?'

Was he playing games at my expense? 'Thanks for the lift. It was very kind of you.' I tugged on the door handle and clambered out, dismayed to find Grandidge had likewise got out of the car and locked the doors.

'It's no trouble. But I'd be glad of a coffee before I hit the motorway.'

'I only have instant in the flat.' I dug in my bag for the door keys. When I'd extracted them I looked up to find Grandidge studying the tree closest to my door, his open palm resting on the trunk. Was he talking to the thing? He turned away and I felt as if I'd somehow been caught eavesdropping.

'Instant will be fine.' He grinned. 'That's a healthy tree, all considered.'

'It's okay, as trees go.' I shoved the front door open.

'You should take more time to appreciate these things. Maybe you'd be less uptight.'

I took the stairs two at a time and jammed the key into the lock of my first floor flat, twisting it viciously.

Grandidge followed. 'Is there someone I could call, so you're not here by yourself?'

'I've got the cat for company.'

'I was thinking in terms of family, friends, significant other?'

I glared at him. 'I'll be fine with the cat. And some peace and quiet.'

The cat chose that moment to jump down from the couch and wrap himself around Grandidge's ankles, purring. Usually he dives for cover when I bring strangers home.

Grandidge picked up the shameless creature, rubbing him behind the ears before handing him to me. 'Kitchen's at the back?'

I nodded and followed him through, clutching the cat, which for once seemed delighted to act as a comfort blanket.

He opened the window and raised the blind so the sunshine streamed in. 'Coffee. You're a coffee drinker, right?'

I nodded. 'There's no need for you do this. I'll be fine.'

'You will, I know. Indulge me.' He found mugs and teaspoons, and dug the coffee out of the cupboard. He looked at ease in my small kitchen. Like he belonged. I had to remind myself he didn't.

'Are you sure there's no one I can call?'

'No, but thank you.' I retreated to the couch with cat and coffee. Grandidge sat for a moment on the couch next to me, then stood up and prowled to the front window that overlooked the street. It was a small flat with not much room to prowl and with even less of an outlook, thanks to the trees.

'Do you have remote access to the work computer system?'

'How else do you think they convinced me to work extra hours?' I set down my coffee. 'Why?'

'I'd like you to check something for me.'

I hesitated. 'That sounds dodgy.'

'Nothing underhand. I just want to see that report.'

'Maddy's bee research?'

'That's the one.'

'That's all?' He should have seen the report anyway.

'That's all.'

I shrugged and booted up the computer. Grandidge continued prowling about until I was logged in.

Calling up the file produced an error message. 'This is odd.'

He leant over my shoulder to study the screen. 'You've found it?'

'No. It's not there. Everything else I worked on that day, the day before, the day after. But not that file.'

'Anywhere else? In your sent emails?'

I checked. 'No. It's gone. Someone with admin permissions must have gone in and removed it. That's all I can tell you. You need someone from IT, they might be able to find a backup.'

He straightened up. 'I'll see what they can do. I'd better get going. Thanks for the coffee.'

He paused at the door. 'We never had this conversation, if anyone asks.'

'I won't lie to cover your back.'

'You won't? I'm wounded.' Then he smiled. 'But no one will ask, you'll see.'

When he'd gone the flat felt too quiet. I crossed to the window, in time to see his car pull out of the end of the street. As I turned away another car followed him out. It was the same colour as the one that had passed by when we arrived. It could be a coincidence, of course. Either Grandidge had found the perfect way to play on my fears or he'd been telling the truth. I wanted John Grandidge to be one of the good guys, but that didn't make it so.

* * * *

The crematorium was packed for Maddy's funeral. I sat at the back, close to the door in case I wanted to make an unobtrusive exit. After all, what business had I sitting there unscathed when I'd been at Maddy's side moments before the collision? It was a relief to escape to the pub afterwards with the rest of the crowd from work and leave her family to their restrained grief. We dealt with it in a more raucous manner and were soon busy badmouthing Harland.

'If I ever catch him alone he'll get payback.' The speaker was a tall, skinny youth, all spots and bluster. If Maddy had ever told me his name I couldn't remember it. 'He always drives too fast.'

'Can't now he's been banned,' an older man from Accounts pointed out. Bob, or Rob, or someone. It wasn't as if it mattered.

'Yeah, well, he'll be back on the roads in a couple of years. It isn't right.' The youth glared at Bob. Or Rob.

I downed my drink. Sitting here growling about Harland with these guys wasn't going to fix anything.

Grandidge came over to sit at our table, loosening his tie as the barman arrived with a tray of drinks.

Bob-or-Rob muttered something about buying company.

Grandidge studied him for a moment; Bob-or-Rob edged away slightly.

Grandidge raised his glass. 'I'm here to give a respected colleague a proper send-off. Will you join me in a drink to her memory?'

We did.

It must have been a couple of hours later when Grandidge poured me into a taxi, then climbed in beside me. 'You're going to have some headache tomorrow.'

'I never get hangovers.' I probably slurred.

'No, of course you don't.'

* * * *

I snapped awake early the next morning with that unnerving conviction I'd made a fool of myself the night before. I took stock: in my own bed and more or less appropriately dressed, if a baggy old T-shirt counted as such. Yesterday's black dress was on a hanger, hooked over the wardrobe door. So far so good. I dragged myself out of bed and pulled on a dressing gown, trying to work out what I'd forgotten. And there he was in the living room, still in rumpled shirt and trousers, unfolding himself from the two-seater sofa as he got to his feet and stretched.

Half-resolved images from the night before chased through my mind. Yes, I'd made a total fool of myself.

'Morning.' He smiled, the sort of smile that reaches deep inside and tugs. 'How's the headache?'

I handled the situation with my usual aplomb. 'I – um – it's fine. You didn't need, shouldn't have…'

'What, the couch? It was a safe distance from your snoring.' He grinned.

I waited for the floor to open up and swallow me, but it didn't. Strange, that.

Sometimes the only way out is through. 'I hope I didn't say anything too stupid last night.'

'Don't worry about it. You were charming. A little drunk, but charming.' He turned to the window and pushed the curtain a fraction aside, peering down into the street.

A vague memory stirred. A car? A car down the street, with two men sitting in it. 'Are they still there?'

'Yes.' He eased the curtain back into place.

'Then they really are following you?'

'It looks like it.'

'But, why?'

'My money's on Harland, looking for ways to discredit your statement about the collision. And digging for any dirt he can get.' He didn't seem unduly bothered.

'Huh?' I stared at him, shutting my mouth after a moment or two. I really knew how to impress a guy. 'I don't follow.'

'Boardroom politics. He sees me as his opponent rather than a colleague. If he can discredit me, well…'

He shrugged. 'You know company policy on staff involvement.'

'A bit rich, given his ongoing thing with Rita.'

'He's convinced I'm out to bring him down.' He grinned.

'That's ridiculous.' My head was starting to thump.

'You think so? I thought it was one of his more perceptive moments.'

'Well, we're not involved.' I wasn't fishing for compliments. I just said the first, stupidest thing that occurred to me.

'True.' His grin widened. 'We should probably work on that.'

* * * *

That summer I spent a lot less time with my cat. It would be fair to say I fell pretty hard. I'd always sworn I'd never get involved with any work colleague, but it was like trying to resist a force of nature. There was something different about John Grandidge. He talked to his plants; his flat was full of them. He would throw the windows open whenever he was home and insects would buzz in and out as if they knew they were welcome.

I even took him home to meet my parents, that's how smitten I was. In one short weekend visit he convinced them both it was time for the family farm to go organic. We drove back to the city full of plans for the future. My only regret during those months was that Maddy wasn't there to give me a hard time over my besotted state.

* * * *

It was a beautiful August morning when Harland took a dive from the fourth floor boardroom window onto the car park. The 29th, I remember the date because at the time I was in a ground floor toilet cubicle, juggling handbag, — the hook was broken off the door, but at least the lock worked — paper cup, and pregnancy test kit, trying to see if the little line had turned blue by the flickering light that Maintenance had sworn they'd replace last Friday.

The outer door banged as someone came into the restroom. My juggling act failed and the not-so-discreetly labelled carton dropped on the floor. I stamped on it, before anyone could read the label. This was one bit of news I had no intention of sharing any time soon.

Had it been long enough? I peered at the white test stick. How long before it should react? I'd stuffed the instruction leaflet back inside the carton, which was now jammed on the floor under my right foot. The light flickered again. Was that a faint blue smudge, or just my imagination?

Oh, fuck.

And then a dreadful hollow 'crump' sound outside the window.

The fine hairs on the back of my neck rose; instinct recognising the sound of sudden death long before reason could catch up with it. I froze, as if the terror might somehow pass me by.

From somewhere in the distance came a prolonged scream; somewhere up above.

Reason caught up again and I tipped the contents of the paper cup down the loo and flushed, stuffing cup and test kit into the waste bin as if I'd been caught out in some kind of wrongdoing.

I dashed out of the side door to the car park: it's next to the Ladies' so I was first on the scene. If this is what the CEO had in mind when he'd insisted all admin staff took first-aid training it had been wasted effort.

The nausea that had been stalking me all week tightened its grip at the sight of his body facedown on the tarmac, blood pooling over the point of the white arrow. The same white arrow where Maddy had died, pinned under Harland's 4x4 on that perfect spring morning, only four months ago.

I turned away before my roiling stomach got the better of me. A woman screamed from above. I looked up in time to see Rita leaning out of the open tilt-and-turn window, which was seesawing crazily. Then she vanished back inside and John's head and shoulders appeared.

'How bad is it?'

I shook my head.

For the most fleeting of moments his expression changed, as if he was pleased by the news. Then the security guard appeared at my side, claiming my attention.

'I've called an ambulance. We should…' His voice tailed off as he realised Harland was beyond any need for first aid.

I took myself and my urgent need to puke back to the Ladies' loos.

* * * *

'So, Miss Carter.' The detective peered at his notes. 'You were in the Ladies' lavatory at the time Mr Harland fell to the ground? Tell me again what you were doing there?

It's clear from the CCTV footage you were in there some time.'

I was peeing in a goddamn paper cup. I told him. I spelled out why in words of as few syllables as possible.

He nodded and scribbled something in his notebook. Then looked at me again, pushing his specs back up his nose. Some guys look good in specs. Trust me, he wasn't one of them. 'And do you know who the father might be?'

'Of course I do.' And it was none of his damn business.

'Well, Miss Carter? It is Miss, isn't it?' He held his pen poised over the notepad.

'It's a personal matter. I haven't had the chance to discuss it with the father yet.'

'A man has died here today. This is a serious matter.'

As if I hadn't noticed. 'Excuse me. I still feel unwell…' I needed to puke again. Now I'd started, I couldn't seem to stop. As I stood up I glimpsed the last word he'd written on his notepad: Uncooperative.

That toilet cubicle was bidding to become my second home. I emerged to find Rita leaning over the basins to use the mirror. She was applying lipstick with intense concentration, obviously suffering the effects of a liquid lunch. She straightened up and glared at me, taking a hasty step back to keep her balance. Her hair was slipping loose from her uptight up 'do.

'You,' she snarled. Really, she snarled. 'Don't think you have me fooled with your Little Miss Nice act. I know what you and Grandidge have been up to. I know what you did.' She prodded an accusing finger at me, swaying towards the door. 'I know what you did. And you won't get away with it. I'll see to it.' She turned and staggered out, colliding with the doorframe on the way through and swearing at someone in the corridor outside.

I washed my hands and rinsed my mouth with tap water in an attempt to feel more human. It worked. Sort of.

I tugged the door open and found John waiting outside.

'Yvonne said you weren't feeling too well.'

'I've felt better.'

'You need a doctor?'

'No. At least…' Maybe there was never a right moment for those conversations. At that moment it was easier to put it off. 'What happened up there in the boardroom?'

He made a gesture of annoyance. 'Still no vote. I've convinced a few we should halt production, but it's one of the company's top-selling products.'

Even besotted as I was I had to admit John's worldview appeared warped at times. 'No, not the bee thing. I meant Harland — what happened? Did he actually jump?'

'Of course he did. Has Rita been telling you I pushed him?'

'Is that what she's saying?'

'She's lost it. I was on the other side of the room when he opened the window and climbed out. And it gets better; she says you were waiting downstairs to make sure he didn't get up.'

That explained the police questions. 'That's ridiculous.'

'Quite. But she's played into my hands at last. There'll be a vote of no confidence in her tomorrow. With her off the board I can push the product recall through. Boardroom politics are so damn slow.' His manner swung between elation and annoyance. Of course people would respond to stressful events in different ways. Or so I told myself.

* * * *

Rita resigned the next day. She never even turned in for work. That night, back at John's flat we celebrated. It turned into a double celebration as he'd already worked out for himself what the serial puking signified. And he was pleased. What's more, now it was out in the open I discovered I was pleased he was pleased.

'It's a good sign. Means your body's adapting well.'

How did he know that? He hadn't studied medicine, as far as I knew. Did he have siblings with children? Or children of his own? I really knew next to nothing about him. He talked to plants and cared about wildlife. Until now it had never occurred to me to ask anything about his background. Maybe it was time for answers to some of those questions; just as soon as the new life we'd created was through making my stomach reject the meal I'd been enjoying.

Pregnancy was already changing my life, starting with a new appreciation for modern plumbing. I was drying my hands and face in the bathroom when the refill valve in the toilet cistern shut off with a clunk. Voices intruded on the ensuing silence. One was John's; the other man's I didn't recognise. They spoke rapidly. The pitch rose and fell as they argued, too far away for me to make out their words. Not that I wanted to eavesdrop. I hesitated, then opened the bathroom door with a clatter and for a moment there was silence. Then a few murmured words and a click of the latch as the outer door closed.

John stepped away from the door as I returned to the living room. Something about his expression told me he'd sooner I'd not been aware of the visitor.

'Did I hear someone at the door?'

'Neighbour. Thought a courier left his parcel here.' He shrugged and turned away to pour himself a whisky. 'You want one?'

'I...probably shouldn't.'

He set the bottle down. 'No, you probably shouldn't.'

Our celebration had been short-lived, unless John drinking himself into a stupor over the next couple of hours counted as a continuation of it. When he passed out on the bed I left him to it.

I roamed about the flat, mind buzzing with the questions I'd never even thought to ask before tonight. There were no answers to be found among his possessions. He had little in the way of personal belongings in the flat at all; if it hadn't been for the plants it could have been a suite in any upmarket hotel.

It was turning dark outside so I crossed over to the window to draw the curtains, pausing to admire the last of the sunlight fading against the city skyline. But the beauty was marred by a niggling unease that someone was watching me. The fine hairs on the back of my neck prickled as they had when Harland died. Chilled to the core, I studied the empty street. It wasn't empty; three figures sheltered beneath the portico of the building across the road. As I looked closer they faded back into the shadows of the doorway, so completely I began to doubt I'd ever seen them at all. I pulled the curtains shut, abandoning any thought of going back to my own flat for the night. Instead I double-checked the door and windows were locked before burrowing under the covers next to John for warmth.

John seemed to have shaken off his dark mood the next morning; at least until I mentioned the figures I'd seen across the street.

'How many of them?'

'Three, I think.'

'Where were they?'

'Down there.' I pointed to the doorway; there was no one there, of course, yet he frowned.

'Always the west.' He didn't seem aware he'd spoken out loud.

'Do you think Rita's carrying on where Harland left off?'

'What? Those two in the car? No. She's not behind this.'

'How can you be sure? She was furious with us. What if—'

'She's history.' He pressed his fingertips to his temples. 'These guys are hardcore. They shouldn't bother you, but…well, don't give them an excuse.'

And he wouldn't tell me any more than that.

* * * *

They were waiting for us in the underground car park: three innocuous-looking men in cheap polyester suits. I didn't recognise them by their faces, but by the familiar chill that crept across my shoulders. I froze at the foot of the stairs, every instinct screaming at me to turn and run.

John squeezed my hand. 'You go and wait for me at the front door. Okay?'

'No. Not unless you come with me.'

'I've no time to argue; just do it.' He gave me an intense stare.

Somehow I found myself releasing his hand and backing away up the stairs, entirely against my will. I caught hold of the handrail and clung to it to halt my progress.

The tallest of the three strolled forwards. 'Johnny, it's been too long.'

John tilted his head. 'You and I both know it's not time yet.'

'And we both know the rules. You've been drawing attention to yourself.'

'I've been getting results.'

'Petty vengeance? That was never part of your remit.' The stranger shook his head in mock sadness.

'You have no idea what it's like here. No idea.' John took a step towards him. 'There's still so much more to be done.'

The stranger drew in his breath. 'Not by you, Johnny. Your privileges are revoked.'

John's shoulders tensed. 'You can't do that.'

With a metallic shriek of protest the nearest car careered against John, shoving him across the access lane and pinning him by the legs against the car opposite. I hurled myself back down the stairs towards him, but the tall stranger stepped between us and grabbed me by the arms.

'Is this her, Johnny? She's pretty.'

'She has no part in this.' John's pain fought every syllable.

'No? Maybe we should bring her along, just to keep you honest.'

I tried to twist loose and he tightened his hold on my upper arms. I've never worked out what happened next; it all seemed impossible. The car pinning John flipped right over into the air and slammed against the other two men. John dived at my captor, shouting a single word as they grappled. 'Run.'

The grip on my arms loosened and I pulled free. I sprinted for the concrete stairs, taking them two at a time, tripping on the first landing and scrambling halfway up the next flight when a massive blast floored me.

* * * *

I woke in a hospital bed.

No one believed me, of course, even though they found four bodies among the burned-out cars just as I'd described. They concluded I must have stumbled into some elaborate insurance scam, which went tragically wrong, despite the fact no relatives came forward for any of the dead men. I soon learned it was wisest to say nothing about certain things. Whoever — or whatever — John Grandidge had been, I kept my thoughts to myself. I told them what I knew, of course, but in truth I knew very little. Much later I learned Rita had committed suicide the day she resigned from the company. And John's certainty she had no longer posed a threat took on a sinister new aspect.

Eventually they ran out of questions and released me with a tentative diagnosis and several bottles of pills. I went home; not to the flat but all the way home, back to the farm. The first thing I did when I got there was head for the bathroom and flush away the pills.

* * * *

The baby's due in a month's time. All the scans have confirmed it's healthy, nothing untoward. At the health centre they tell me it's perfectly normal for a first-time mother to be worried. I nod and tell them as little as possible.

I struggle to recall in any detail much of what happened last year. Sometimes I remember a face, or a fragment of a half-forgotten conversation. But some things I'll never forget, however hard I try. I feel safe here, and that's all that matters. It's the right place to raise John Grandidge's child. The window faces west. The barley field stretches away down to the river and the road skirts the edge of the open field. I can see anyone coming long before they can see me. And I'm certain about one thing: when they come, they'll come from the west.

Blame The French
Stephen Gallagher

The pub was called The Antigallican, but everyone knew it as The Ship because of the picture on the sign.

In its day it was a relatively respectable, end-of-the-street, no-frills working-class tavern with a men-only snug and brassware in the lounge. Shift workers would call in on their way home, and at weekends put on a collar and tie and bring their womenfolk. In the long summers, we children would sit out on the pavement with crisps and lemonade while our parents were inside. The landlord had a dog named Charlie.

The building still stands, but the sign's long-gone and it's been boarded up for ages. I'm here to tell you about the night that closed it down.

It was decades after my Dad had taken me there for my first pint and I was making a few bob as the weekend potman, clearing up glasses and stacking them for washing. Times had changed, the work had gone, and the area had the worst of the town's declining fortunes. Apart from the Gardening Club that met once a fortnight with free sandwiches, the main clientele consisted of solitary old men drinking themselves to death, and young thieves.

Eileen and her husband had run the place as a couple. After he left her, she kept the license and ran it alone. Things stayed much the same for a few weeks but then she moved in a lover who, at twenty-two or three, was half her age. His name was Kieran and he knew a good thing when he saw one. He and his mates made the place their own. I don't know if boys like him are born with the looks of a thug, or what process shapes them if they aren't. He was long-limbed and skinny, with a bony-hard skull and small, squinty eyes. A dangerous weasel of a boy, and I don't mean just screwed-up squinty. He'd one eye so badly turned inward that it might have been comical, if the look of it wasn't so terrifying. No one ever commented on it. Of his mates, I think only two of them had jobs.

Early one Friday evening I was setting up chairs and mats when the first customer of the night came in. I looked twice because I'd never seen him before, and we got very few strangers. At first glance you'd have thought he was homeless: the Big Issue-selling kind of homeless, not the ones who beg. His hair was long like a sixties hippy's, his beard similarly untrimmed, and the coat he wore was one of those long German Army parkas that can be had cheap on the market.

I called up the stairs to Eileen and he stood with his hands on the bar, looking around, waiting until she came clattering down to serve him.

"What can I get you, love?" she said, unlocking the cash drawer under the optics, showing no reaction to his appearance.

"Pint of best," he said, and his voice was low and a little raspy. "Please."

He counted out the money in small change. His hands were filthy, the nails bitten right down. Eileen pulled the pint, let it settle while she banked the coins, then topped it off. One thing about her, she looked after her beer. He took a sip from his glass and then cast another glance around the lounge.

By now Eileen had relocked the till and gone back upstairs, and it was just him and me. I tried to guess his age. I couldn't. He was probably quite young.

"Something's changed," he said, and he nodded in the direction of the dartboard on the wall. "There used to be a picture. Right there."

"Are you from around here?" I said.

"I just remember the picture," he said.

"You mean the old sailing ship," I said. "The Antigallican. Same one you see on the sign. They moved it into the snug to make space for the darts. Everyone wonders about the name. It means – "

"I know what it means," he said, and he took his glass over to the door of the snug and pushed it open.

"Suit yourself," I said as it swung shut behind him. At that moment there was a burst of loud music through the ceiling from upstairs. Eileen shouted something and it was cut off as abruptly as it had begun. Kieran at home, was my guess.

I went about my business. So he didn't care for my stories. Antigallican means "enemy of the French". Why anyone would want to make a pub name out of that, I've no idea.

When I'd done, I looked over the counter and into the snug, which had a small counter of its own on the other side of the bar. I couldn't see the stranger. Behind me, some of the regulars had begun to arrive. They came in alone, and they'd mostly sit in silence. I called up to Eileen and then went through into the back room to see what was what.

He was sitting across from the picture, contemplating it as he drank. It was nothing special. Not an original. Not even a very good print.

I said, "You might want to sit somewhere else."

He looked at me. "Why?"

"Frank likes to sit there. Frank's a regular." I didn't add that Frank was also a day patient who talked to himself in a bitter, incoherent tirade.

He didn't seem impressed. "There are plenty of seats," he said.

"That's what I mean," I said. "You can sit anywhere."

"So can Frank," he said.

He didn't move. I leaned in and said, in a low voice so Eileen wouldn't hear, "You don't want to risk trouble. Frank's touchy. And this isn't one of the good pubs."

"It used to be," he said, and returned his attention to the picture.

Well, I'd done what I could. I went back into the lounge and left him there, sipping his warm beer and watching a listing ship on a flash-frozen sea, going nowhere.

Kieran's friends turned up a short time after that. Four of them, the main gang; drooly Doug and stupid Steve, and the one who worked in the park for the council, and the one who'd been sacked from Kwik-Fit. They must have called him up as they were walking toward the door because Doug still had his phone in his hand and Kieran appeared just as they entered.

"Where've you all fukkin bin?" he said.

"Fukkin town," said the failed Kwik Fit fitter.

They always behaved themselves around Eileen, paying for their drinks and knowing better than to annoy her, though when she was out of sight they'd lean over the bar and top up their own glasses from the pumps. The first time I caught them, Kieran said, "I told them it's all right." After that, they'd catch my eye and grin at me while they were doing it. Did I ever say anything? No I did not. I was only the potman. And whatever soft spot Eileen had for her thick-as-pigshit squinting stud boy, I wasn't going to risk trespassing on it.

That evening they gooned around and every now and again one of them went outside with his phone where the signal was better, and the place filled up as much as it ever did on a Friday night. At one point Kieran disappeared upstairs and came down with a Macbook hidden under a towel. Origin unknown, but it wasn't hard to guess; some student's bedroom, or a momentarily unattended bag in the middle of town. He showed it around, but no one wanted to buy. He took it into the snug and came out a few moments later; making the kind of face you make behind someone's back to ridicule them. The stranger was still alone in there.

A hen party came in and brightened the place for a while, half a dozen of the local chip-fed beauties meeting up for a taxi on their way to the clubs. The boys tried to flirt, but the girls were too sharp, and their powder was reserved for better prey.

Then Frank showed up.

I don't know what Frank's exact problem was, or what had led him to this point in his life. Eileen had barred him a couple of times, but he kept coming back. He was a cursing machine, low and under his breath and entirely self-directed. She'd eventually realised that the drink calmed him, and that the best thing to do was to let him settle in his corner and self-medicate. After twenty minutes or so he'd go quiet and for the rest of the evening he'd be docile.

"Hey, Frank," Kieran shouted across the pub. "You know there's some fukker in your seat? Says he'll fight you for it."

Eileen was in the back changing a barrel, but she came running at the shouting and the sound of breaking glass.

Everyone piled into the snug behind her. By everyone, I mean me followed by Kieran's gang, who came along more as eager spectators than useful supporters. There was beer on the floor and broken glass underfoot.

Frank was sitting quietly. He was trembling and the stranger's hand was on his shoulder. It was hard to say whether it was a grip of reassurance or whether the stranger was holding him down.

The stranger was looking at me. "You didn't tell me he was troubled," he said.

Kieran said, "You. You're barred. Get out."

"I say who's barred," Eileen said sharply, and Kieran shut up.

The stranger looked down at Frank and said, "He wasn't always like this." Then he released the older man's shoulder. Frank stayed put. He didn't look up. He was in his usual seat, now.

The stranger looked at Kieran and said, "Are you the one who tried to make him fight me?"

"So?" Kieran said.

Eileen said, "Did you?" And he flushed and said, "No."

She didn't bother to call him on the lie. She said, "Clean this up while I get the man another drink."

"Me?"

"You heard."

He just stood there, and Eileen lost patience with him.

"Oh, for fuck's sake, Kieran," she said. "Start earning your keep."

"I don't work here."

"You don't work, full stop. It's time you did something useful."

The stranger said, "Sounds like one of us has to go."

Kieran snorted and started to glance around to share the moment with his mates, looking for solidarity at the same time.

"I'm not going anywhere," he said.

His mates all seemed to agree that going anywhere was an unlikely option under the circumstances.

"Are you a sportsman, Kieran?" the stranger said.

"What do you mean?"

"You've been all mouth so far. Stirring up trouble and throwing your weight around. But can you back it up?"

"I can fukkin take you," Kieran said.

"Only if you want to see this woman lose her license," the stranger said. "If you want me out of here, let's make a bet for it."

Kieran didn't know what to make of this. The stranger looked at Eileen. "He's not your son, is he?"

"No," she said. I couldn't quite tell if she was amused or offended.

"Is there anything he's good at? If he wins, I'll clean up the mess and leave. If I win, he's the one who has to go. What happened to the pool table?"

"The brewery took it out when it broke," she said. "There's just the dartboard now."

"I can manage darts," the stranger said. "A bit rusty but, you know. How about it, Kieran?"

"Darts?" Kieran said.

"Arrows. Don't you play?"

One of the others spoke. "Go on, Kieran," he said. "You can chuck arrows."

"Well, now I'm worried," the stranger said, although he didn't sound it. "You understand the bet. If I lose, I clean up here, walk out that door, and never come back. If I win, you do the same."

"I'm not cleaning up."

"You're missing the point. You don't just clean up, you clear out. For good."

"But I live here," Kieran protested, and looked to Eileen for support. I enjoyed the expression on his face when he found none. She was looking at him with a spectator's interest.

At that point, someone started making clucking noises. Like a chicken. We all looked around. They were coming from Frank. He didn't look up. But I'd never seen him smile before.

That did it. We all went through into the lounge and a couple of Kieran's friends cleared the tables away from under the board. The house darts were produced from behind the bar. It was a brass set with Union Jack flights, in a green plastic box with a cracked lid.

The board was like some rotted cork float that spent years in the sea. The wood had been picked away and only the wire held it together, so heavily had it been used. But it would serve. Kieran had his confidence back now, and while I hoped to see him thrashed, I didn't expect him to honour any outcome that went against him.

However, something had changed in Eileen. The novelty of Kieran's company must have been wearing thin. He and his friends stole so much from the bar that their custom can't have been an asset. She was a middle-aged woman, unexpectedly single. Everyone had a good idea of why she'd taken Kieran in. His looks and personality had little to do with it.

Sometimes there's a moment in your day when the worst junk food is just what you need. But that doesn't mean you'll feel good about it afterwards.

"You go first," Kieran said, and held out the arrows.

"How do you want to do this?" the stranger said as he took them from him. "Three darts, highest score?"

"Whatever."

I saw a look pass between a couple of the yobs. Kieran had all the unproductive status skills of the urban youth. He knew pool, pinball and platform games on his mobile phone. He might never read a book, but the nudges, holds and bonus functions on a slot machine were no mystery to him. At the dartboard he'd screw up his wonky eye like Popeye and he had a weird, little-finger-out throwing motion that looked odd and effete, but he tended to hit what he was aiming for.

The stranger squared up to the throwing line.

"Highest score with three arrows wins it, then," he said. He raised a rock steady hand and sighted down the dart. I didn't like how close Doug the drooler was standing behind him.

And I was right, because as the stranger threw, Doug body-bumped him and spoiled his aim. The arrow ricocheted off the edge of the board. The stranger turned and Doug just smirked, secure in the numbers behind him.

Eileen said, "Take that one again."

And the stranger said, "My own fault. My hand slipped." But he stared Doug in the eye until Doug moved back, trying to pretend that moving was his own idea.

The stranger squared up to aim again. He had only two darts now and I didn't see how he could hope for a winning score with such a disadvantage. Why had he refused the chance to void his mis-throw? It was Eileen's pub. She could set the rules and no one was going to argue with her. I could see her eyes tracking the stranger, wondering what he was about. The boys, unable to imagine much beyond the obvious, imagined nothing but his impending humiliation.

Frank had joined us to watch. That was a first. And he was silent, which was another.

The stranger said, "I once asked my dad what Antigallican meant. He said that a soldier who came home from the Napoleonic Wars saved up his pay to open an alehouse. It was his dream. He called this place The Antigallican to commemorate his service. But you know the irony? He'd brought home a French wife. After he died, she wouldn't change the name."

The second arrow hit with a thunk and went in deep. It was a clean throw, straight and forceful. Top half of the board, just right of centre.

"Life can be strange," he said.

Score one. One point. And I'd swear it was exactly what he'd been aiming for.

The boys all hooted and Kieran said, "That's it. Pack up. Fuck off."

"I still have one throw," the stranger said. "And then it's your turn. A lesson for you, Kieran. It's not actually over until you've counted the score."

83

He looked at Eileen. Eileen's expression didn't change. Then he raised his last dart and started to aim.

The entire pub was silent.

As if to draw out the moment, he said, "This morning I went to see the house I grew up in. All those memories. And what did I find?"

We all waited to hear what he'd found.

"Cockroaches," he said.

He turned as he threw. The arrow flew straight, but it wasn't toward the board. I saw it cross the room and slam into its target.

Which was Kieran's good eye. Yep. Right in, to the hilt. I heard him gasp and his hands flew up. They stopped inches short of touching the dart, which was now firmly planted in his face and wasn't about to fall.

"Your throw," the stranger said.

Kieran started making a sound. It grew louder. His hands were flapping around close to his face, wanting to pull out the arrow but not daring to touch. His other, inward-turned eye must have had the perfect view.

The sound he made was hardly human.

Everything kicked off then. The people at the back of the pub made for the doors. Kieran's friends made for the stranger, and the stranger jumped over the bar. There was a hard wooden baseball bat kept underneath, hung in a special bracket made by a previous landlord, and the stranger knew exactly where to reach. He came up swinging and took Doug down with his first, drove one of the others back with his next, and I think the one after that broke somebody's arm. I grabbed Eileen and pulled her over to the wall, which was about all that I could do.

The police didn't take long to arrive. It was an area they knew too well, and there was always a car within speeding distance. By then Kieran was sobbing, holding a bar towel to his face as he waited for an ambulance, and Eileen was giving first aid to the one with a broken arm. One of the others was throwing up in the Gents and the fourth one had disappeared. There was a growing crowd on the pavement outside. I don't know where Frank went.

The stranger had returned to the snug. I looked in and saw that he'd kicked the broken glass aside and was sitting, once more contemplating the ship on the wall. The Antigallican. He'd drawn himself a fresh pint.

I said, "Navy?"

He shook his head.

"Special Forces?" I watch a lot of those films.

No.

"What, then?"

Out in the next room, paramedics were trying to move Kieran and he was getting hysterical.

"Just a local man looking for a quiet drink," the stranger said.

The Silence Between The Sounds
Scott Harrison

I

Every night the dream is the same.

It is an hour after dusk and Master Melchior is sitting in the sand on the edge of the encampment, legs crossed, his back resting against one of the slumbering camels, watching the stars fall from the sky.

He is blind, of course; the eyes having been plucked from his head a long time ago. And yet somehow he still knows that I am there. He turns his head as though looking at me and the sockets are deep, swirling craters of blackness.

"Mures'Sia Proxima has gone hypernova," he tells me, softly. Then he smiles and looks away from me, turning his face towards the inky twilight that seems to encircle the encampment.

Somewhere, out there, the young girl is struggling in terror as she is held down in the sand, trying desperately to break the Trinity's grip and flee into the night, as the man steps forward, sword in hand, ready to sever the limb and cauterise the ragged flaps of skin with a flaming torch.

I can hear her screaming; terrifying, animalistic sounds, that immediately make me think of the goats they used to slaughter in the marketplace during the Feast of the Great Silence; a terrible mixture of desperation and finality, of complete and sudden understanding.

Master Melchior reaches forward and snatches a handful of sand from the ground at his feet, allowing it to pour out slowly through his clenched fist. And I can hear it shushing through his fingers, can feel each and every grain tumble through the air in a desperate bid to be free of the man's grip and be lost amongst its brothers once more.

I look down and for the first time I realise that I am a child again of five or six summers, witnessing my first Blooding Ceremony.

Scared now, I turn around, desperately searching for my parents, hoping to catch a glimpse of faded scarlet robes somewhere amongst the untidy knot of onlookers that have gathered before the fire. But I know, even before I look, that they are no longer there. They have taken the Trinity's money and gone. By now they will have mounted their horses and be heading back to the village.

Sold to the Magi, just like I was all those years ago.

Then the screaming stops, and suddenly it is all over. The ancient steel blade has done its work and the girl is now lying calm and silent in the sand, her eyes fixed upon the Trinity as they wash the blood and clumps of skin from the sword.

"It's finished," Master Melchior announces and he opens his palm to show that it is empty, all the sand now gone, returned to the ground at his feet. As he does so the eastern sky begins to lighten, the stars falling faster and faster, until the area around us becomes as bright as day.

It is starting all over again.

A new Incursion.

I can sense it in the air; a bitter, sulphurous tang hanging low beneath the smell of burning flesh and salty blood.

"Must we make the journey again, Master Melchior?"

I know that he can hear my words, yet he does not turn to face me, instead he places his head in his hands and weeps.

For a long moment there is silence.

It is only when the chaos begins – as it always does in this dream – that I wake to find the pale dawn light creeping in through the window of my chamber.

I am an old man again. Some seventy summers have passed since my first Blooding Ceremony and now I am tired and alone and oh so very frightened.

There is only me left now. No one else. Just me.

But, even so, I know what I must do; I have done it so many times before, been making this journey and performing the same rituals since I was a pale youth barely off my mother's tit. Never alone though. Never has it been just me. Before there had always been the Trinity. The Magi.

And yet, even though I know that I am too old to face the power of the creature – that this time it will surely kill me, just like it did the others – I do not hesitate in my actions. Instead, I calmly and methodically bundle up my belongings and strap them securely to the camel's saddle.

Soon I am ready for the journey to Bethlehem.

II

The Desert of Judea – 1BC

There it was again. The briefest flash of ivory, burning fiercely amongst an endless sea of bronze. There for just a second or two, then gone.

"Riders," Caspar muttered, as he slid carefully down from his camel. "Herod's men, come to see what we're about."

Balthazar scanned the desert around him in silence for a moment, before wrinkling his nose in disgust. "Scabrous dogs. I'm surprised it has taken them this long. By my reckoning we're well within the borders of Herod's kingdom."

"Crossed it five miles back, easily," I agreed.

I glanced behind me, expecting Melchior to still be seated on his camel, but he had dismounted the moment we'd stopped, and was now standing alongside Caspar's animal, one hand resting on its mighty flank, staring off towards the horizon, towards the approaching riders. As I watched he tore a short strip of cloth from the hem of his robes and tied it across his dark, eyeless sockets like a blindfold.

"They're here for the same reason that we are," Melchior said in a low voice. "Only Herod doesn't know it yet. He feels the danger, but has no understanding of it; cannot comprehend what it is. Not yet."

Melchior sighed and I waited for him to continue. When I realised there would be no more, I said, "Do we go on? Meet them further along the plateau?"

But it was Balthazar who answered my question. He drew his sword and, holding it like a dagger, drove the blade down into the sand in front of him. When he stepped back the protruding weapon looked like some gloriously ornate, golden cross glinting in the harsh afternoon sun.

"We stop here, for now. This place will make as good an encampment as any." He pointed eastwards, towards the shade of a clump of date palms that overhung a small, shallow oasis. "Bed the camels down over there while we prepare for the Giving."

I did as I was told, taking each of my masters' animals by the reins and leading them into the cooling shade of the palms. Once they were fed and watered, and they had settled themselves noisily upon the ground, I stripped naked and washed myself in the cold, oasis waters. When

I was finished, I wandered slowly back to the spot where the camels were resting, and sat beneath the thick canopy of leaves with my eyes closed, allowing the gentle afternoon wind to dry the water from my skin.

I must have dozed briefly, for when I opened my eyes again the ritual of the Giving was over, and Herod's riders were approaching the encampment.

The four men dismounted from their horses one stade from where we had made our camp and fell into an immediate huddle, as though trying to decide amongst themselves if they should approach or just shout their message from where they stood.

I climbed to my feet and dressed quickly. After a little time Master Caspar appeared at my side and placed a hand lightly upon my shoulder, the trace of a smile on his lips.

"These men are mindless fools who follow a desperate king; we must be on our guard at all times. Remain silent until they are gone. Only Melchior will speak with them."

I nodded my understanding, then we turned our back on the animals and joined the other Masters.

Soon the whispering was at an end and the soldiers of Herod appeared to come to a reluctant decision. First they unstrapped the heavy sword belts from their waists, letting them fall into the sand at their feet, then slowly, painfully, they shuffled forward towards the Trinity.

The four men came to a halt at the lip of the camp, refusing to come any nearer, choosing instead to stand and square their shoulders aggressively, glowering down at us as though expecting a surprise attack.

"You are the *Magi*?" the one at the front spat the word out as though it tasted like camel shit. It was obvious from the coloured sash that hung from his shoulder that he was nothing more than an ordinary juda; although from the looks of him he probably favoured a more grandiose title, such as chancellor of the guard or first captain.

Melchior smiled at the man benignly, ignoring the hatred that crouched behind the bastard's words like an assassin.

"We are the Trinity," he confirmed, with a slow nod of his head.

The juda dragged his contemptuous gaze across us with great suspicion, then asked, "This is your entire company?"

"This is all that we are," Melchior told him. "The three Masters, our bondman, and the animals over by the oasis. There are no more."

At the mentioning of camels, the juda's attention flew hungrily towards the tiny pool of water, a keen fire burning in his eyes, his manner like that of a Great Desert Hawk sizing up its prey.

"Fine looking animals," he said at last, voice flecked with avarice. "They would do well for the King's menagerie."

"You are Herod's juda?" Melchior asked.

The word had an immediate effect upon Herod's man, for he tore his eyes away from the resting creatures and stared down at the old mystic in fury.

"Watch your mouth, you eyeless bastard," he spat. "I am a captain, in charge of over fifty of the King's personal guard. I am here to find out why a caravan of whores is knocking at Herod's door."

Melchior shook his head slowly. "Your master did not send you all the way out here just to find out what we were about. If the stories of Herod are true then he knows full well what our business is. And, what's more, he will be as worried as we are."

The juda did not reply immediately. Instead he took the time to look us over again, one by one; his eyes lingering on me the longest.

"Ah, but you are a sorry looking bunch of horses' backsides," he barked. "Why would the King allow the likes of you to travel across his kingdom?"

"Because he knows that we are the only ones who can stop the Incursion." And here Melchior kissed the palms of his hands and touched them lightly against the thin material stretched across his sightless eyes, in the same way he did whenever he spoke of the Great Incursions. "Without us he is a dead man."

"Is that a threat, shamen?" the juda asked.

Suppressing a chuckle, Melchior said, "A statement of fact. It was the Trinity that saved his grandfather's life, and his great-great grandfather before him. It is the time of Ouroboros, when the serpent devours its own tail and the wheel of history turns full circle."

The juda jabbed a finger in my direction. "What about him? Is my master to believe that some smoothed-skinned whelp who has not yet learned to shave is to save him from the Endless Night?"

"What your king chooses to believe is his own affair, I could not care less either way," Melchior said, plainly. "The fact of the matter is either he allows us to pass through his land unmolested, or the whole world will be swallowed by eternal darkness."

III

We were made to wait in a small anti-chamber to one side of the throne room for what seemed like an age before Herod finally granted us an audience.

The old stone hall was cold and vast and, for the most part, empty; a handful of palace guards stood listlessly about the room, looking bored and disinterested, barely glancing up as we were brought before the King. Only the juda of the guard, who stood like an obedient dog beside his master's throne, watched us as we entered, his eyes burning with barely concealed anger and loathing.

Herod sat silently for a moment, waiting for us to prostrate ourselves before him, but my masters remained resolute, unmoved, standing before the King with an air of calm indifference.

After a second or two of awkward silence, Herod gestured vaguely at the juda beside him, who immediately leant across and whispered something in his master's ear.

"My captain here tells me that you intend to cross my lands to the east," Herod said at last.

"We beseech your Majesty that you grant us safe passage, nothing more," Melchior said.

"He also tells me that if I do not do what you ask of me then I am a dead man."

This amused my Master. "It would appear that you have a fool for a captain, your Majesty," he said. "For he has taken my words and twisted them until they hold no meaning."

The juda began to protest, but a gesture from the King silenced him.

"I hope that what you say is true, otherwise it sounds to me like a threat," Herod said.

"I merely told him how important it was that we remain…uninterrupted…on our journey," Melchior told him.

Herod pursed his lips, considering my Master's words carefully. "The Great Incursion," he said at last. "I too have seen the signs. My grandfather wrote many books on the last such occurrence. I have read them all."

"Then you will understand the importance of our task," said Melchior.

"Can it be stopped, do you think?" the King asked.

At this Melchior only shrugged "If we are to learn such a thing, then a blood sacrifice must be made," he said, plainly.

The King stiffened slightly, obviously troubled by the mention of a sacrifice.

"And who will be this sacrifice of yours, shamen?" Herod asked.

Melchior remained silent for a second or two, the ghost of a smile fluttering across his lips, then he turned and rested an old, leathery hand upon my shoulder.

"Matters of sacrifice are not my domain," he told the King. "Such dealings fall within the province of my bondman."

With only the slightest of movements the King beckoned for me to step a little closer to the throne, eyes narrowing in mistrust as they flicked restlessly across my face.

"And what do they call you, *bondman*?"

He spat the word from between his wet, bloated lips as though it was a title of great honour that, as far as he was concerned, I had not yet earned.

From somewhere behind my right shoulder Caspar snorted with laughter, causing Herod's face to twitch in annoyance.

"Before I was given to the Magi I was known as Amahl Damji," I told him. "But that person died long ago and bondman Karsudan now stands in his place."

"So tell me, bondman Karsudan, will you be the one to condemn an innocent man to a slow and agonising death?"

"I will, your Majesty," I said quickly. "The deed must to be done for our work to be successful; it's as simple as that."

"And who must we sacrifice in order for your *voudou* to work?"

Without hesitation I pointed towards the man standing at his right hand, the self-proclaimed captain of the King's guard. "We must have the life of the juda or the Trinity's gift will not be yours this day."

At first the juda snorted in derision at my words, but this quickly melted away into horror when he realised that Herod had no intention of standing in the Trinity's way.

As the man was dragged away from the throne, towards the very centre of the stone hall, Balthazar stepped forward. "He will not suffer, your Majesty. The killing stroke will be a swift one."

But Herod only shrugged. "Swiftly or slowly, I care not. Kill him how you will, shamen, his life is not worth a rat's fart to me."

After the juda had been stripped, bound and gagged, Caspar read the Rite of The Blooding while Balthazar disembowelled the man alive; his movements were darting and quick; the knife-blade flashing in the light from the flaming torches as it tore through the air, then through grimy skin and muscle.

When the words were spoken and the flesh was suitably torn, the Trinity stepped back from their work and bowed their heads in silent worship. At their feet the juda thrashed violently in an ever-growing pool of thick, scarlet liquid, the heels of his feet pounding at the dusty flagstones as he tried desperately to drag himself to his feet.

In one swift and final movement, Balthazar thrust the Blooding knife through the dying man's throat, pinning him to the stone floor, at once transforming his screams into wet guttural rasps as he gasped his final breath.

As the light in the juda's eyes started to fade…

…the visions began…

…and there was a voice saying…

"…the stars are falling and the remnant has come."

It is Master Balthazar's voice, but where it comes from I cannot tell, it is too dark to see clearly.

"Yet, even that word 'remnant' does not describe the thing adequately," Balthazar again. "This is so much more than just the remains of the last Incursion, this is something new, something that never was before."

"These words you speak are meaningless," Herod's voice this time. "You sound like a market-place soothsayer."

"Have patience, your Majesty. At the moment there is nothing for us to read but echoes and confusion. Give us time, the meaning will become clear, you'll see." This response comes from somewhere behind me. It is my Master Caspar.

There is an explosion of light from somewhere high above and the first of the stars begin to fall, streaking down through the darkness as if they were bleeding from some gaping wound. And in the pale light I can see the dim figure of Herod crouching in the sand beside me, his hands raised before his face as though he were trying to shield himself from some terrible, unseen attacker.

"What horror is this?" Herod calls over his shoulder. "Are we witnessing the end of all things?"

"Not an end, your Majesty," Balthazar tells him. "But a beginning – what will happen if the Incursion is not stopped."

Then, just beyond the jagged peaks of the distant mountains, a star slams into the earth, causing the ground beneath our feet to tremble and shake. For a second or two fire belches from the crater like a mighty volcano, and an unspeakable shapeless horror can be seen writhing and twisting at its core.

"Look, there! See it?" Melchior's voice is flecked with fear. "The Incursion is successful."

And all at once my Master Melchior falls to his knees and begins to sob, his head thrown back so that his face is to the heavens, hands clawing desperately at the pale sand beneath him.

"Bitter exile! Banished to dwell within the stranger-lands! No more to live as the silence between the sounds, but forced to take dreadful, solid form! Cursed to exist!"

The voice he speaks with is no longer his own; the one he uses now seems dead, lifeless, without inflection or emotion; a mocking parody of Man's sacred tongue.

"I am to become real, to become living. But if I am to suffer then so too must every living thing. Where I walk there will be no day, no night, only the eternal darkness, the endless howling vacuum of nothingness."

Somewhere in the distance a church bell chimes out the hour of midnight and I know it to be that of the Church of Our-Lady-of-the-Path in Bethlehem.

Herod knows it too, and with wide eyes stumbles backwards in the sand, trying to get away from the kneeling form of Master Melchior.

"No!" the King shouts. "No, I want this to stop, now!"

And suddenly the air fills with Heavenly singing as though the people of Bethlehem are rejoicing, celebrating the coming of this new Incursion.

"Stop this!" Herod shouts again, or, rather, tries to.

But the singing does not stop. Instead it is getting louder and louder, and the King's voice is becoming lost beneath the ululating wave of sound.

And then Herod no longer has a voice, his mouth flapping silently open and closed like a landed fish dying on the banks of a river.

And the singing is almost deafening now, the air vibrating around us as the voices continue to rise in pitch.

And Herod tries to scream again…

…and again…

…and again…

…and where Herod lay, the early morning sunlight bathed the stone floor with brightly-spun gold. The King glanced about his throne room in disbelief for a handful of seconds, as though doubting what his own eyes, his own senses, were telling him.

"It…it is morning," he said, at last.

It was not a question, more a statement of cold, hard fact, but Caspar answered him anyway. "Aye, your Majesty."

The King swallowed, wetting a very dry throat. "How many days were we entranced?"

"Not days, merely hours," Melchior told him. "The vision was a deep one, but thankfully relatively brief."

With great swiftness my Masters Caspar and Balthazar darted forward and grasped Melchior by the arms, helping him to his feet.

"Hours?" Herod echoed the word as though it held little meaning for him.

Caspar gestured towards one of the high, arched windows situated at the farthest end of the throne room. "Aye. This light you see is the dawn of the twenty-fourth day."

"Then all that we have just seen…?"

Melchior shook his head slowly, his expression thoughtful. "It has not happened yet. But it will."

A deep, ponderous silence followed, during which time Herod dragged himself painfully across the room, before flopping down onto his throne with a troubled sigh.

After an irresolute pause he said, "Can you…can you stop it?"

But my Masters remained silent.

IV

There is a small town somewhere to the west of Tulkarm, huddled along the banks of the Mediterranean sea, called Senecca. It is not very well know, in fact, I have never met another living soul who has heard of the place other than myself, but nevertheless there it sits at the very edge of the calm blue ocean, and has done so for at least three centuries.

They know me there, or at least, they knew me many summers ago when I was younger, when I was part of the Magi, the Holy Trinity.

I used to have a woman there, a tall, raven-haired laundress named Fasiya, who would feed me and fix my clothes and even take me to her bed when she was of the right mood. She knew what I was and what I would become in time once my apprenticeship was served and she did not seem to mind.

And for this I almost loved her.

One evening after we had eaten and made love, we lay naked and sweating in the cloying, still heat of midsummer, listening to the distant waves crashing against the sand. I was just beginning to stumble into a fitful doze when suddenly and without warning Fasiya sat bolt upright on the bed next to me, as though something had alarmed her.

I opened my eyes and in the half-light I could see her sitting over me, her long hair falling untidily about her shoulders as she regarded me with those intense, dark eyes.

After a few minutes like this she took my hand and said, "When the time is right I want you to ask your Masters to take Wadi."

Wadi was her son, then only three summers old; the only thing she had left that belonged to her late husband. Sadiq had died eighteen months earlier when his fishing boat had foundered against the rocks in a violent storm. Not long after, Fasiya had been forced to sell all his possessions, and now there was nothing left to prove that the man had ever existed in this world…except for the boy, Wadi.

I propped myself up on my elbows and regarded her closely, all thoughts of sleep now gone.

"That's not my decision, Fasiya," I told her. "Such selections are made by Balthazar."

"Then persuade him," she said simply.

This made me laugh. "You don't persuade a man like Balthazar. He can be a stubborn old bastard when he wants to be."

"Ah, but you're forgetting that I know you only too well, Karsudan. If anyone can talk their Masters round it's you," Fasiya said.

I consider her words for a moment, then said, "But why would you want to give up the only thing you have left of your dead husband?"

"Because this way he will have a future," said Fasiya.

At this I shook my head. "I wouldn't count on it."

"If he stays here what life will he have?" she asked. "Spending all his hours at sea for a meagre pittance, just so that others will have fish to fill their bellies? If he doesn't fall overboard and drown he'll be dashed against the rocks just like his poor father."

"And he might not," I said. "You may find that he enjoys working on a boat like his father. He may even have a good life; marry some beautiful, slender, raven-haired woman, have fifteen children and die a happy man while rutting himself stupid at the age of seventy."

"No one else in Senecca is happy. Why should he be any different?" she asked.

"Because he's your son and you should be doing everything in your power to make his life different from everyone else's."

"I am. That's why I want the Magi to take him," Fasiya said.

"But he could die, Fasiya!" I said plainly.

"Don't you see – so could they!" Fasiya reached out and gently ran a fingertip along the ridge of scars that crisscrossed my chest. "The Trinity could die, Karsudan, and leave you all alone. Then who'd be there to help you if there was another Incursion?"

"I'd manage," I lied.

Fasiya shook her head. "No. No you wouldn't. But with Wadi there to look after you…well, then you might."

I told her that I'd think about it and Fasiya left it at that.

That night I slept fitfully and the dreams, when they came, were filled with blood and death and eternal darkness.

We were in Bethlehem.

V

"All three of us must die," Balthazar told me plainly. "There is no other way."

The air crackled and a flash of light lit the darkness around us as we came to a halt outside Our-Lady-of-the-Path; it was clear that we had but a short time before the Incursion would begin, but exactly how long there was no way of knowing.

I turned to look at the frightened crowd that had begun to gather on the other side of the small dirt road and I knew then the terrible price that would be paid should we fail. At the very front of the group a young boy, no more than four or five summers old, was cowering beneath the robes of his mother. His hair was of the finest, light brown and his eyes were as black as the night sky as they sparkled and shone in the lightning flashes of coldfire.

And just for a split second I thought of the boy Wadi… and of his mother, my dead beloved, Fasiya.

Despite the sharp stab of fear gnawing at my bowels and belly, I knew what I had to do. Drawing my sword I moved forward, intending to take my place alongside my Masters, but upon seeing me Balthazar's face creased into a disapproving frown.

I felt a gentle hand upon my shoulder, halting me in my tracks, and I turned to find Caspar standing at my side.

My old Master shook his head sadly. "Not you, Karsudan. Put your sword back in its place. This is not your battle. Your time will come, but this is not it."

"But I should be by your side," I told him quickly. "If you are to die then that must be my destiny too."

And then I heard another voice from somewhere deep inside me, *The Trinity could die, Karsudan, and leave you all alone. Then who'd be there to help you...?*

"Your destiny is four days' ride from here," said Caspar, and he pointed a finger towards the low ridge of mountains in the west. "In the city of Dakash, as we agreed."

"But, Master…" I began, but got no further.

There was an explosion of light from somewhere high above, turning night-time into brightest day, and the first of the stars began to fall, just as my Master's vision had decreed.

"Mures'Sia Proxima has gone hypernova." Melchior told us with a great sadness in his voice. "It is time for the beginning to end and the end to begin."

Caspar's hand gripped my shoulder tighter then, and he pushed me away from him, towards the waiting party of camels.

"Go, Karsudan. Take the animals and go to Dakash. This is not your fight, you have no business here."

At first I refused to go, simply standing there dumbly with the reins of my animal clutched in my hands, staring back towards my Masters as they readied themselves for the fight.

Then Melchior pointed the tip of his sword in my direction and said, "We leave the future of mankind in your hands, Karsudan. You are no longer an apprentice, you are all that is left of the Holy Trinity. When the time comes you will know what to do."

And with that they turned and strode away down the street until, one by one, they became swallowed up by the darkness.

I turned and clambered up onto my camel, then quickly galloped out of Bethlehem, a train of empty animals following in my wake. I did not stop until the town's outer walls were a handful of stades behind me and I had reached the top of the first hill, then and only then did I allow myself to climb down out of the saddle and stand looking back across the valley towards Bethlehem.

For a long moment there was only silence.

Then, without warning, there was chaos.

VI

But all that was such a long, long time ago.

I was so very different then.

If you were to look upon me now, you'd see me for what I truly am…

VII

I am a lonely, foolish old man; tired and scared. I do not want to do what I have come here to do, but I don't have any choice in the matter. There is no one else.

Just me.

I am all that stands between the peoples of this world and the yawning pit of eternal darkness.

So Fasiya was right, after all.

For the past sixty-nine summers I have been known only as Karsudan, but that is not my true name. No. I was born Amahl Damji, in the city of Dur-Sharrukin, the only son of a stonecutter and a seamstress, sold to the Magi against my will on the day of my fifth birthday.

I no longer feel like the Karsudan of old, no longer feel like I deserve to carry that name. When I wash, the empty, hollow eyes of a stranger stare back at me from the surface of the water; when I shave, it is not with the steady, purposeful hand of the youth I once was, but with the uncertain hand of an old and tired fool. When I sleep the bad dreams come and they are filled with blood and death and eternal darkness.

I am not the same man that I was all those years ago, yet I make the journey, nevertheless.

I have no choice.

When I arrive on the plateau, Balthazar's sword is still there, exactly where he left it, protruding from the sand like some ornately carved, golden cross, glinting dully in the afternoon sun. The oasis is just as I remembered it, too; the date palms a little taller and thicker, perhaps, the line of water sitting lower against the shore.

This seems as good a place as any, so I set up camp.

Taking each of the animals by the reins, I lead them into the cooling shade of the palms, just as my Masters had taught me so long ago. Once they are fed and watered, and they have settled themselves noisily upon the ground, I strip naked and wash myself in the cold, oasis waters. When I am finished, I wander slowly back to the spot where the camels are resting, and sit beneath the thick canopy of leaves with my eyes closed, allowing the gentle afternoon wind to dry the water from my skin.

I must have dozed briefly, for when I open my eyes again it is night and the first of the stars are falling from the sky.

"It is time for the beginning to end and the end to begin," I say, remembering Melchior's words.

I drag myself painfully to my feet and wander slowly back towards the camp. As I do the eastern sky begins to lighten, the stars falling faster and faster, until the air around me becomes as bright as day.

It is starting all over again.

A new Incursion.

I can sense it in the air; a bitter, sulphurous tang hanging low beneath the smell of warm sand and animal shit.

"I must make the journey again, Master Melchior," I suddenly say aloud. I know that he can hear my words, even though I have not seen his face for fifty summers or more.

Then I place my head in my hands and weep and for a long moment there is silence.

It is only when the chaos begins that I know what I must do.

Clutching the rusting hilt of Balthazar's sword I draw it from the sand.

I am a lonely, foolish old man; tired and scared. I do not want to do what I have come here to do, but I don't have any choice in the matter.

There is only me left now.

No one else.

Just me.

Containment
Justin Richards

Wednesday was crop circle day. Most boring day of the week, right in the middle. But after Wednesday – after the crop circles – the weekend was in sight.

I cover the whole county, and most of its countryside. Open, rolling, green, and superstitious. I get some reports of witchcraft, some hens that won't lay or cows that are giving sour milk. There are the usual unusual lights in the sky (nothing at all to do with the RAF Base at Fullavon, oh dear me no), and of course crop circles.

Actually, I don't mind the crop circles. When I first started, I got a bit hung up about them and wondered if they might actually be evidence of alien visits. Then I met old Henry Macallister and he laughed and choked on his cigarette smoke and bought me a drink he was so amused. After that he took me out into one of his fields with a ball of string and a plank of wood and we spent a cold but illuminating few hours creating one of the most impressive crop circles I'd ever seen.

So now I know. Now I don't look up at the sky above the field and wonder. I look round the gathered locals and watch for the suppressed smile.

And that Wednesday was just like any other. I reckoned I had the probable culprit in my sights while the poor old farmer shook his head and some local woman muttered about witchcraft and the dead spirit of Miss Agnew whose headstone never did stand upright in the churchyard.

There was a silence you could cut with a scythe, if you happened to have one handy. Or, I guess, if you were the Grim Reaper having a bit of a laugh. And in that silence the theme for Scooby Doo rang out loud and clear.

Seeing the expression on the face of my prime suspect, I elevated him from probable to definite and answered my mobile. 'Detective Sergeant Shane Andrews, can I help you?'

It was the chief, wanting to know how I was spending such a glorious sunny day, and whether – if I had a few moments – I could possibly spare the time to join him and a few of his colleagues at the docks back in town where there was a bit of a situation and he would welcome my help. Well, he didn't phrase it quite like that, but you get the gist.

'That was my spirit guide,' I explained to the gathered locals. Several of them looked impressed. Several of them laughed. Most looked sort of bemused. 'Anyway,' I went on, 'I have to get back to town where my police colleagues can't manage without me, apparently. So, just to set your minds at rest, I can exclusively reveal that this crop circle we are standing in was most certainly not the work of any human.'

'You can tell that?' the farmer asked, impressed.

'My spirit guide informed me.'

'By phone?'

I shrugged. 'It comes with the job. So does the Scooby Doo ring tone, before anyone asks.'

'So,' someone else said slowly, 'if it wasn't a human that did this..?'

'My spirit guide tells me that this is without doubt the work of that feared alien entity, known as…' I clapped my hand down on the prime suspect's shoulder. 'Phil Dexter.'

Funnily, young Mr Dexter was the only one not laughing now. I decided that it was time to leave them to sort out whatever compensation was appropriate – probably derived from apples and measured in pints – and I set off towards my car.

At least, I thought I did. But finding your way out of a field of corn that's as tall as you are isn't as easy as finding your way into it. Eventually I got back to the road, and soon after that I found where I'd left the car. It's not a patrol car; I mean they don't want to advertise that they have a full time officer assigned to supernatural occurrences. Even if they do call it 'Miscellaneous Duties' and pretend they've got a whole department doing it. I have to provide my own transport. But at least it means I can smoke in it. I don't smoke – never have. But I could. And in a job like mine every little bit of freedom is a victory to be savoured.

So I made my non-smoking way back to town, singing along to something tuneless from the eighties and wondering what could be so weird that the Chief wanted me to see it, and so urgent he'd phoned me himself, and so important he'd used a phrase like: 'Get your backside here within the hour or you'll be helping old ladies across the Clembury Road until you retire without a pension, probably very soon.'

* * * *

I could tell it was big as soon as I got to the docks. There's a security gate that wouldn't keep out a determined eight year old, but I stopped dutifully to flash my badge at the bored geezer wearing a cap three sizes too big.

'You'll be wanting Block Three, Area G,' he told me.

'Ah, that'd be over there would it?' I asked, pointing across the sea of containers waiting to be shipped in or out. 'Where the ambulances, police cars, scene-of-crime unit and plastic tape is. Just by all those blue flashing lights.'

He nodded, impressed I expect with my deductive powers and keen observation. Or something. Well, like I said – I'm a detective.

It was these same incredible powers that alerted me pretty much immediately to the fact that things were not good. Never mind the ambulances, I could see the Chief standing just inside the tape cordon, talking on his mobile. And his face was green. Well, not green green, but green. Sickly, pale, shocked.

I parked where there was space, and made my wary way over towards the cordon. Not wary enough though, as the Chief spotted me and abruptly ended his call. I braced myself for a tirade, for the accusations of being late and wasting my time out in the sticks, for the insults and recriminations.

'Thank God you're here, Andrews,' he said.

I wobbled a bit, but managed not to pass out with shock. 'Glad to help, sir,' I told him thinly.

'You won't be when you see what we've got.' He held the tape up for me to duck underneath, and led me past grim-faced silent uniforms. 'Got us stumped. You're our last resort.' He attempted a smile to show he wasn't being as rude as this sounded. But his face wasn't used to smiling and it didn't really work. I think the relevant muscles have sort of atrophied or forgotten what to do under such extreme circumstances.

Not that I cared a few moments later when I saw where he was taking me. Mind you, I could smell it before I saw it.

'What is that?' I said out loud.

'Don't ask,' the Chief told me. 'I've never seen anything like it,' he added encouragingly. 'And I hope I never see anything like it again.'

There was a container in front of us. One of those huge corrugated metal things they load on the back of a lorry and use specially to clog up the motorways. The end of it was actually two huge doors. One of them was standing open. Inside I could see that there were bright working lights set up on metal tripods. The forensics boys and girls were there in their white overalls. They're a hardened lot in forensics. They've seen it all, and can handle anything.

One of the forensics guys came out of the container and leaned heavily against the closed metal door, heaving in great gulps of air. He looked… Well, let's just say it wasn't the most encouraging sight.

'What's going on? What's in there?' I demanded. I wasn't going another step until I had some sort of warning.

'Illegal immigrants,' the Chief said. He'd veered off to one side and it was quite clear he wouldn't be coming into the metal container with me. 'We got a tip off. It's not unusual. The poor souls are crammed into a shipping container with nowhere near enough water or food and left pretty much to fend for themselves. They're lucky if they don't suffocate in there.'

The Chief was looking round as he spoke. He pointed across to where a young woman was sitting on the ground, her back pressed up against another of the containers. 'That's Britta Hutchinson. She was here before us. Works for the port authority. Doing a spot check. They like to be sure what's coming in is what it says on the docket.'

'Guessing it wasn't,' I said. 'Guessing she found the illegals.'

The Chief nodded. 'It'll take her a while to get over it. If she ever does.'

'Get over what?' I hazarded.

'She opened the container. Found them inside. Dead.'

'I sort of gathered,' I told him. It was hardly a surprise. And it obviously wasn't pretty. 'Dehydration?' I wondered, remembering what he'd said about water.

'No,' he said. 'Take a look. Then tell me what the hell happened in there. Because no one else here has a clue.'

* * * *

I walked into the container, and almost walked straight out again. Almost walked straight up to the Chief, and handed him my badge there and then.

Except, between you and me, I don't have a badge. Not really, not like those American police you see in the movies and on TV. They get badges – and guns, and uniforms that fit... I got a plastic card with a magnetic strip, which is supposed to open security doors at the station, and let's be fair sometimes it does. There's a picture on it. Don't know who it is – some distant relative of mine, maybe. There's a vague similarity. If you angle it right. And squint a bit.

But that was an 'almost'. What I actually did was find a spare bit of space to stand in and close my eyes and try to hold my breath.

When I opened them again, it was all still there. Had it been better, or worse, I wondered for Britta Hutchinson? I'd been warned there was something nasty in the container, but she'd come across it unsuspecting and alone. There again, she'd have seen a glimpse, in the dark. I was standing there with the harsh lights set up by forensics, surrounded by people dressed entirely in white.

If only that had been all I was surrounded by. But there were the bodies. Or parts of bodies. Or… I shuddered, not really sure what I was seeing. Anatomy was never a strong point – at least, not when it isn't all in the right place and still warm and alive and surrounded by skin.

Someone handed me a hanky. Maybe it was just a piece of cloth. But whatever it was, I clamped it over my nose and mouth as I forced myself to look round at the carnage. At the bodies of all those poor people ripped and torn apart.

'We haven't got it all catalogued yet. So please try not to tread in anything,' someone said.

Which did it for me. I turned and stumbled back towards the doors and fresh air and sanity and the real world.

But hey, I never miss the chance for a witty comeback. So as I went, I turned to shout something back to the guy. Can't remember what it was now, which is tragic as I'm sure it was the wittiest, most come-back-y comeback ever in the history of witty comebacks.

Instead, I slipped on something I'd rather not think about and definitely won't be describing in detail, and went flying. Which was probably less impressive, if rather more amusing.

The end result was certainly more useful. I landed on something soft – no, not describing that in detail either. With a shriek of embarrassingly shrill surprise and disgust, I rolled off the mortal remains of a dark-haired woman dressed in shredded clothes. Wasn't only the clothes that were shredded, either. But I barely noticed that, thank God.

Because I was busy fighting to keep my breakfast in place as something under the mutilated body moved.

I watched in fascinated horror as a head appeared. A tiny, misshapen head. Wiry dark hair cascaded like wool from a sagging scalp. Its eyes were unnaturally large, with stitches round them. Like a caricature of humanity, an approximation of a little girl. A small, pudgy hand lifted towards me. A hand with no fingers…

I almost shrieked again, which would have been even more embarrassing. But just as I was thinking that this creature, whatever it was, looked bizarrely like a child's doll, I realised that this was because actually, it was a child's doll.

And that the child who was holding it – the small, terrified girl who'd escaped whatever hell had unleashed in this metal tomb by hiding beneath the mutilated body of a woman who might even be her own mother – was watching me through dark, terrified eyes.

'It's all right,' I said quietly. 'It's all right. It's all over.' I tried to smile reassuringly, which probably frightened her even more. Then I was pulling myself to my feet and yelling for the medics, the forensics team – anyone and everyone.

* * * *

The little girl didn't say much. And what she did say, none of us understood. She didn't seem injured, miraculously. She clutched her loosely stuffed cloth doll with its big dark eyes tight as the medics gave her a quick check. Then they bundled her into an ambulance.

They took the young woman who'd opened the container as well. Shock, the Chief said. Well, I think we'd all had a good dose of that. So I decided hospital was probably the best place for me too, and I left the forensics teams to their forensicsing.

'I want answers,' the Chief told me as I got into my car. 'Not half-baked stories about vanishing demons or anything like that. Proper answers.'

'Me too,' I assured him. I love crosswords. And I was hoping Britta Hutchinson could help me fill in a few blanks, at least until we found a translator who could tell us what the little girl had seen. 'I think,' I said seriously to the Chief as I started the engine, 'that we can rule out the doll.'

Leaving him with that thought, and a rather pained and unforgiving expression, I drove off after the ambulance.

* * * *

They'd settled the girl in a small private room. From what Britta Hutchinson told me, they reckoned the container had come from Krejikistan. Which meant it wouldn't be easy or quick to find a translator.

Britta was in the next room. In fact it was really only a flimsy partition with a curtain across that separated the two beds. Hospitals can't even afford decent walls these days.

'They'll just keep you in for a few hours and then check how your blood pressure's doing,' I told Britta. I knew what I was talking about – I'd asked the doctor on the way in.

There wasn't much value or point in talking to the girl, who was (a) traumatised to the point of almost total silence and (b) didn't speak any language I could understand anyway. So I settled myself into an uncomfy chair for a nice chat with Britta. There were a few advantages to this. First she spoke my language. Second she was actually rather attractive – with a bob of dark hair and just about everything a young lady should have in the right positions, proportions, and appearance. Last, and probably least, she might actually be able to help me with my enquiries.

'So how are you feeling?' I asked her, cutting to the quick of the investigation. 'Can I get you anything?'

'Not too bad,' she said. 'It's just, the shock – you know?' Did I mention she had almond-shaped eyes, rather like a cat? No? Probably not important then. They were a deep and gorgeous green. Just so you know.

I nodded sympathetically. 'I saw inside the container. And I'd been warned. It must have been…' I let my voice trail off. Actually, I couldn't begin to imagine how it must have been. 'Why don't you tell me what happened?'

She shrugged, or as close as you can get propped up against a mass of pillows. 'We check the containers, at random. Just pick a few to see they're carrying what they're supposed to be.'

'Which in this case was what?'

She shook her head. 'Don't even remember. Engine parts, I think.'

I nodded as if I knew everything there was to know about engine parts, which isn't technically the case. 'Go on.'

'I'd checked a couple of other containers. It was just me. Sometimes Customs come round with us, but not this time. I opened the container, and…' She turned away.

'Not good,' I said quietly. 'Not good at all.'

'I couldn't really see at first. It was the smell.' She turned back to face me, looking paler now. 'That awful smell, you know? And I went in, and…' She shuddered at the memory. 'Got blood all over me. I staggered back out, just as a police car arrived. They said they'd had a tip-off about illegal immigrants. What happened in there? What happened to those poor people?'

'I don't know,' I confessed. 'Not yet.'

'Will you ever?'

'Yeah,' I assured her, sounding far more confident than I felt. 'Soon as we get a translator, that little girl can tell us all about it.'

'The container was locked. From the outside.'

'So whoever it was that did this locked it behind them,' I said. 'Look, they were probably killed days ago, on the ship. Forensics will tell us soon enough. It's all pieces of the puzzle. Don't worry,' I told her, 'we'll get whoever did this.'

She nodded, smiling thinly. I think I'd reassured her. 'When will you find out? How soon can you talk to the girl?'

'Well she's even more shocked than you are,' I confessed, glancing at the partition and the curtain. 'And there's the language problem.'

'Quite a while then.' I could hear the disappointment in her voice. 'I just want to know.'

I stood up, putting my hand over hers reassuringly on the bed cover. We both looked at it – streaked with mud and grass stains.

'Sorry,' I said. 'Been in a field all morning. Crop circles.' I grinned to show that I wasn't embarrassed and that I was an expert in just about everything. Not sure she was convinced. 'But anyway,' I went on quickly, taking my countrified hand away, 'we can get the bare essentials fairly quick, I hope. I'm going to get a pad and some pencils from the shop down the corridor. She might not be able to describe it in words, but our little survivor can maybe draw us a picture of what happened.'

* * * *

I heard the screaming as I was on my way back, barely five minutes later. Now, I'm not an expert in hospitals but even I could tell that this sort of screaming was way above the norm. Even if they had a dental department.

And there was another sound mixed in with the screams. A growling, roaring, animal noise. Not normal at all.

The other thing I worked out pretty fast was that the noise was coming from the small private ward where I'd just left Britta and the little girl. Clutching the coloured crayons and pad of paper I'd bought – I guess in case they came in handy either as weapon or means of defence – I ran.

There were other people running too, though most of them seemed to be heading the other way. Which was probably sensible. I pushed through, and barged into the door leading into Britta's room. I was yelling, hoping to frighten off whatever was in there. Or just possibly scared witless. Whatever.

The bed was empty. The covers were ripped and torn. The pillow was lying on the floor in shreds.

I barged through the partition door and skidded to a halt.

The little girl was cowering in the corner of the room, crouched down beside the bed. She was clutching the cloth doll in front of her.

Beside her was Britta. She looked round as I came in, then turned quickly back to the small girl.

'It's all right,' Britta was saying. 'It's OK. You're safe now. We won't let anything happen to you.'

'Is she OK?' I asked.

'She is, yes.'

I didn't need to ask what Britta meant. Because, though I haven't mentioned it, there was someone else in the room. One of the junior doctors I'd spoken to when I came in earlier and who had examined the girl. He was lying on the floor, and he was in the same sort of shape as Britta's pillow. Only more messy.

'I think I frightened it off. Whatever it was.' Britta was still trying to comfort the girl, who was sobbing, clutching the doll tight to her now.

'Did you see..?' I gasped. The shock and the adrenaline were kicking in. Along with the fact I was totally unfit

133

and had just done a twenty metre dash in double-quick time.

'I heard…' Britta shook her head. 'I don't know what I heard. I called out, came running. And found…' She gestured at the dead man lying behind her.

'Lucky you did,' I said. 'Whatever was in here tried your room next.'

The room was suddenly full of nurses and doctors. A woman in a suit was trying to calm the little girl – and doing about as well as Britta had.

'Let's get her out of here,' I told the woman.

At the sound of my voice the girl turned. Her dark eyes fixed on mine for a moment. Then she pushed the woman out of the way and dived under the bed to avoid Britta. She resurfaced a moment later on my side and ran straight at me.

I thought she was going to knock me flying. But instead she enfolded me in an enormous tight hug. He whole body was shaking and she was sobbing again. Through the sobs she was saying something over and over again. I couldn't really understand it, but it sounded like 'Vrolak'.

'What's she saying?' I asked Britta.

She shrugged. 'No idea. Is it important?'

'Doubt it. She's not safe here,' I announced, but I don't think anyone was listening, except Britta. 'Neither of you are. You get home and stay there,' I told Britta.

'Is it because of what we've seen? Or might have seen?'

'Got to be a possibility,' I admitted. The body of the young doctor looked like it had been treated the same way as the poor people in the container. It didn't take a genius – or a detective – to make a connection.

'What about the girl?' Britta was asking. 'She can come home with me. Until you can get a translator.'

It was a kind offer. I'd have accepted it at once except the thought of how much paperwork might be involved scared me as much as the ripped up body being stretchered away. But I had no idea what the alternative might be.

So it was something of a surprise to hear myself announcing calmly: 'No, she's my responsibility. She's coming home with me until I'm sure she's safe and we can get a translator.'

I gave Britta my card, with my mobile and home numbers scribbled on the back – for strictly professional use, of course. The girl was tugging me away, as if she'd understood what I'd said and was anxious to be going.

She pulled away from Britta as the young woman walked past us to get to the door. The poor child didn't seem to want anyone near her except me. I've always been good with kids. Well, good-ish. Well…

Anyway, this kid was still clinging to me as I led her through the maze of corridors to the car park. She was still muttering 'Vrolak' over and over. Something like that, anyway. I wasn't paying that much attention to be honest. I was staring at the list of car park charges, working out how long I'd been there and how anyone could ever afford to get ill. Maybe that was the idea – keep the waiting lists down by charging people out of the whole hospital market.

'Come on,' I said encouragingly to the girl. 'You and your dolly are going to be just fine.'

* * * *

The poor girl was in her hospital gown of course. She was still saying 'Vrolak' over and over, like I should understand what she was on about.

In return, I held up a finger, hoping she'd guess I meant I would be back in a minute. She watched me nervously as I closed the door on her, locking her inside my tiny flat. Then, praying she was at home, I went down to Mrs Collett on the floor below.

I don't think she really believed my sob story about my little niece coming to stay and losing her bag on the train. But she lent me some of her younger girl Imogen's pyjamas, t-shirts, jogging bottoms and underwear.

'Thanks,' I said, taking the bag from her. 'The poor girl's exhausted; I left her having a nap. I'd better get back.'

'Bring her round for a play with Imogen,' Mrs Collett said.

'Yeah, right – good idea.' Probably not such a good idea to explain my niece doesn't speak a word of English, I thought. 'Not sure how long she's staying though.' I thanked her again and ran back to my flat.

Like I said, it's tiny. Only one bedroom – so I'd be sleeping on the small sofa in the cramped living room. There's a little kitchen off that. Then there's a tiny box room and a surprisingly spacious bathroom. And for some reason a space-wasting corridor contrives to run between all the rooms. I call it the hall, but that makes it sound a bit posh and grand. Like they say, there's no place like home.

I gave the girl the pyjamas as it was getting late, and showed her the bedroom. I couldn't be bothered to find clean sheets and duvet cover but I reckoned she'd cope for one night. Then tomorrow I'd call the Chief and decide what was the best for her. Best, and safest. She wolfed down two plates of beans on toast (gourmet chef, me). While she was eating – still clutching her doll with one arm – I tried to find out her name. But still all she would say was 'Vrolak'. Between yawning. She must be exhausted, I thought. Anyway, it was a bit of a relief when my mobile rang.

Even more of a relief that it wasn't someone from work wanting to know what the hell I thought I was doing harbouring a witness. Or whatever. It was Britta.

'I wondered if the girl was OK,' she said.

'Hungry,' I told her, taking the phone out into the hall. 'Otherwise fine I think. I told her about borrowing clothes from downstairs and she was polite enough to seem amused.

'How's the communication going?'

'I think I'll leave trying to get her to draw anything till she's had some sleep,' I said. 'But she keeps going on about Vrolak, whatever that is.'

'Could be anything,' Britta told me. 'Maybe it's her name.'

'I don't think so. Anyway, once I've got her settled I might Google it, see if anything comes up.'

There was a silence for several seconds at the other end, then Britta said: 'Have you got a bottle of wine?'

'Yes,' I admitted. 'Several.' I wondered where this was going.

'Good. That'll save me bringing one with me. I...'
She hesitated, then said quickly: 'I could do with some company. After today. It's been, well – stressful to say the least.'

I couldn't disagree with that. I gave her my address and she said she'd get a taxi. Wondering if I actually had two intact wine glasses, I went back to the kitchen to see how the girl was getting on with her second helping of beans.

The beans were gone. And so was she.

'Hello?' I called. I hadn't seen her leave the room, but I'd been a bit distracted on the phone. The bathroom door was open and she wasn't in there. With increasing anxiety I hurried to the bedroom.

And found the girl snuggled up under the duvet, her cloth doll clutched tight to her chest. She opened her bleary eyes, and smiled at me.

'Good night,' I said. 'Sweet dreams.' She was fast asleep before I'd stepped out of the room.

Not being sure how long it would be before Britta arrived, I opened a bottle of decent red wine, and decided I'd better test it properly. The first glass seemed to work all right, and since there was still no sign of Britta I decided to perform a further test, just to be sure.

Armed with a full glass, I headed for the study. Did I mention I had a study? I probably called it the box room. Which it is. But as well of the boxes I've not got round to unpacking since I moved in (er, seven years ago… or possibly eight) there's a small desk with my state of the ark computer on it. It's not actually driven by steam, but not far off. Anyway, the 'study' is the room right at the end of the hallway.

While the machine was taking its usual forever to get warmed up and do whatever it is computers have to do before they're ready for human beings to get involved, I went back to the lounge. I lit a couple of candles left over from the 1850s or thereabouts (probably) and dimmed the lights. My little lounge now looked exactly the same, only darker. I left it to its own devices and returned to see how the computer was doing.

It was just about there, so I fired up the web browser and waited for Google to load. Typing in 'Vrolak' got me a list of hits. Most of it was film reviews or YouTube stuff. Boring and irrelevant.

But half a dozen pages in, it turned Cyrillic. No idea what language was showing up, but if there was an Eastern European connection to, say – to pick a wild and random example – Krejikistan where the illegal immigrants had come from, then it was probably worth a look.

Except of course I couldn't read the language. For an insane moment I wondered if I should wake up the little girl and see if she could read it. But if she could that wouldn't help me – and depending what the web pages actually said it might not do her much good either.

I scrolled through a couple more pages of incomprehensible lettering and unhelpful things and was about to give up and shut down when I saw something that looked like it might actually be useful.

The search results gave only a heading and a short extract. But the heading was 'Legends of the Vrolak' and the extract read: '… or Vrolak is widely-feared in the lowlands of Krejikistan in particular where the creature is still believed to exist. While there is no scientific proof for…'

Well, there are results and there are Results, and this looked to me like a Result. So I clicked through to it. It was a page of a website about legendary creatures and demons put together by someone called 'Professor Colin H. Stemper'. If it wasn't for the present circumstances (well, and the wine and the low lighting), I'd have had a little bit of a laugh and shut down the computer.

I wasn't laughing even a little bit as I read quickly through the short section about the Vrolak of Krejikistan. 'Vrolak' means wolf, and we were talking big-time nasty werewolf creature here. Something that attacked in the dark and ripped its victims to shreds before feeding on what was left. Something that was massive and dangerous and unstoppable, and that didn't wait for the full moon to get its teeth into you.

The Vrolak was infectious like a werewolf, but for some reason traditionally assumed to be usually female. I glanced towards the hallway, and the half-closed door to the bedroom.

At the bottom of the screen was a heading: Defence against the Vrolak. With a shaking mouse-hand I scrolled down. I expected to find out about crucifixes and silver bullets. But what it actually said was: 'The only known defence against the Vrolak is the so-called wolfstain. This is said to be a lichen-like plant peculiar to the lowlands of Krejikistan. It is not thought to grow anywhere else in the world.'

It might as well have added: 'And there certainly won't be any growing anywhere near you, sunshine.'

In fact, maybe it did. Because I stopped reading at that point. Partly because I heard the sound of a door slamming, and partly because moments after that all the power went off. Including the computer. Including the lights.

As I sat there in the near-darkness marvelling at the strange power of coincidence and coming all too rapidly to the conclusion that this was not a demonstration of that power, I could hear something moving round in the next room.

The next room was the bedroom. Probably just the little girl from Krejikistan where the monsters come from, I told myself. Probably needs the bathroom or is scared of the dark, or…

At this point half my brain was telling the other half not to be so stupid, while the other half was screaming at the first half to get the hell out of there. Being a rational, brave, detective, I ignored the screaming and felt my way down the hall. There was some light from the candles in the lounge. Flickering shadows seemed to be mocking me, but I knew exactly where I was going – oh yes. There was a box on the wall just inside the front door, and when I opened that I'd be able to put everything right again.

To my undeniable relief, when I opened the box and felt along the row of little switches, I found the main trip switch had gone. Probably my ancient computer had overloaded it. I reset the trip, half expecting it to cut out again immediately. But the lights glimmered back on in the study behind me and I heard the hum of the heating cut back in.

'It's OK,' I called. 'Nothing to worry about.' But whether the girl could hear me, or understand from my reassuring tone what I was on about I had no idea. I didn't even know if she'd noticed the lights go out. But I had heard her moving about, so I went to check. The light was on a dimmer switch, and I turned it right down before switching it on, then gradually turned up the brightness so as not to disturb the girl if she was asleep.

I needn't have worried. Not about that, anyway.

The bed was empty. But more than that – it was a mess. The duvet was ripped to pieces, and the bottom sheet was slashed to ribbons. Claw marks, more than an inch apart... Lying in the middle of this carnage was the cloth doll. Its head was missing, and the brown straw stuffing was poking out through the neck and the rips in the body. One leg dangled pathetically by a few threads.

I backed slowly out of the room.

I'd left my mobile in the kitchen when I was faffing about with wine glasses and candles. There was a phone in the lounge, which was marginally closer. The little girl could be anywhere.

Walking as quickly as I dared and as quietly as I could, I made it to the lounge without incident. OK, it's only about ten paces but it felt to me like a major achievement to get there in one piece. And I mean literally 'in one piece'.

The candlelight cast spiky, grotesque shadows across the pale walls. I looked round quickly. The room seemed empty, so I hurried to the phone. It was on a little table out of the way by the window. And it was completely dead. No tone or signal or anything.

A shadow fell across the doorway from the vague light outside. It must be the lamp still on in the study, I thought. Something paused in the hall outside. I could see the large shadow, but the shape of it was indistinct. I could hear the snuffles and heavy breath though. It sounded like a large dog. Or a wolf.

I was motionless, not daring to breath. What might have been a huge, shaggy head turned slightly as if the creature was looking into the room. But I was too far across from the door for it to see. Unless it came inside.

Instead, the head turned away again and it carried on down the hallway. It was heading towards the front door and I hoped and prayed it was going to leave. If the thing walked out of my flat and I never saw it again I didn't mind how much paperwork I'd have to get through to explain and justify it.

But it wasn't making for the front door. It was making for the fuse box again. With a very final-sounding 'thunk' the lights went out and I was left standing in the flickering light of the candles wondering why it was that cops in the USA have guns and just because of geographical bad luck I didn't.

All I had to hand was a large wooden bookend that might make a passable club. I used to have a pair of them, but that's another, arguably less interesting, story. Not that a second one would have helped, as I was keeping my left hand free for the torch I knew was in a drawer under the bookcase and which I hoped had some working batteries in it.

I'd just managed to tease the drawer open as quietly as possible and retrieve the torch when I heard the sound of a footstep behind me. Without thinking, I raised the bookend and turned, swinging my arm down at...

'Britta?'

She looked at me, pale and nervous in the guttering candlelight. 'What the hell is going on? Why don't the lights work?'

'What are you doing here?' I countered.

'You invited me, remember? The front door was open, I saw the light in here...' She seemed to realise how nervous I was looking, and that I was still holding a makeshift club ready to hammer someone's brains out. 'What's going on?'

'Vrolak,' I said. 'Remember?'

She shook her head. 'What about it?'

'It means "wolf" and its loose in the flat.' As I said that, I wondered if it was. 'The door was open?' I asked.

'Yes. Well, just ajar really.'

'Maybe it has gone,' I murmured.

'I don't know what you're talking about.'

'Wait here,' I told her. 'Or better still, stick with me. Safety in numbers, right?'

She didn't answer. At that moment there was a sound from one of the other rooms. Something falling, or a door closing... Something.

'The girl!' Britta exclaimed. And she ran.

'No – wait!' I was right after her, but my foot caught on a chair leg and I stumbled and fell. As I fell, I knocked the table and one of the candles toppled and went out. The other was still giving a smouldering light; enough for me to get myself to my feet and stumble for the door. I turned on the torch as I went and it gave out a weak light.

The torch seemed stronger in the hallway. I could hear the growling coming from the study at the far end of the hall. The lights were out in there now. The growling grew from a low rumble to a sudden roar of sound. I ran down the hall, torchlight waving over the floor and walls.

Britta was backing out of the room ahead of me. She turned, her eyes wide with fear and her hands covered in blood.

Behind her, the little girl followed Britta out of the study. Her pyjamas were ripped and bloodied and I caught myself wondering how I'd explain that to Imogen and her mum. Assuming I ever got the chance.

'Stop her!' Britta was yelling at me. 'You've got to stop her. She's a maniac.'

'Vrolak,' the girl said, her voice sounding like a low growl. She clutched the severed head of the doll in front of her like a talisman.

Britta clutched my arm as I reached her. 'For God's sake, hit her – smash her head in. Kill her!'

It did seem like the only option as we stood there facing her. But – a little girl? I swallowed and drew back my arm. 'Now, hold it there,' I told her. 'Don't move. Not another step.'

'You can't reason with a Vrolak!' Britta insisted.

Maybe it was something in her voice, but I knew that she was right. I remembered the container full of dead people, that Britta had opened. I remembered the dead doctor in the hospital, the little girl huddled in the corner and Britta standing close by. I thought of the ripped bedsheet – the distance between the clawmarks. I could see the girls' fingers clutching the head of her precious doll and I knew.

No way were her hands big enough to make those marks. No way would she rip up the doll that she so obviously loved and needed.

I swung the bookend as hard and as fast as I could.

But a massive hairy paw intercepted it, knocking it from my grasp and along the hall. Britta's face contorted in rage, tufts of hair erupting from her cheeks. The shape of her face was changing, and I could hear the crack of her bones as they moved and warped. Her whole body seemed to grow and distort. Her fingers were claws, her legs swelled and tore through her trousers. Her whole body was covered in thick, dark hair. And just as I thought it couldn't get any worse, her lips seemed to peel back to allow an enormous jutting snout to erupt from beneath. Massive jaws snapped together hungrily, and viscous saliva dripped on to the threadbare carpet. She was transforming as we watched. Into a huge wolf.

Now I was the one backing away along the corridor, wondering what else I could use for a weapon. The torch was shaking in my hand, so that I saw the creature in moments and glimpses rather than as a whole. Which was probably worse.

'You thought you'd get away with it,' I said, my voice shaking as much as the torch. 'Kill the girl – the last witness, and you'd be OK. You opened the container and killed all those people. But the police got there before you could close it up again and escape. Then at the hospital, the doctor found you and I came back before you could kill her.'

I was backing down the hall towards the front door at the other end. If I could get there, I could maybe lure the creature away. Maybe the girl could escape, at least. Or hide, though I couldn't think where since my flat was pretty much full of large hairy wolf and the only way out was down this hallway. But eventually – somehow – maybe she could tell someone what had happened.

My shoulder caught on something. The fusebox. Without looking, I pulled it open and reset the main switch Britta had tripped. I glanced away for a split second. When I looked back, the lights snapped on. And the wolf was hurtling through the air towards me as it finally attacked.

Rough hairy paws closed on my throat. Yellowing teeth came at me and – I admit it – I screamed. I hammered at the great shaggy head with the torch. The glass over the bulb shattered. The paws released their grip just slightly and I tore myself free, falling headlong backwards down the hallway.

The wolf was towering over me. Not at all dazzled by the lights. Jaws open, teeth bared, grinning with triumph.

And suddenly the girl was there. Somehow she managed to squeeze between the wolf and the wall. She threw herself at me – not an attack, but a hug.

'Vrolak!' she said urgently.

'Yeah, I sort of worked that out,' I gasped back, detective that I am. Even breathing was painful.

The girl turned to face the wolf that was bearing down on us both, and incredibly, it took a step backwards. The girl walked towards it.

'No,' I tried to shout, but it was more like a hoarse whisper. 'Run – get out of here. Fetch help!'

But the girl stood her ground, clutching the torn head of the cloth doll tight for comfort.

The wolf-creature leaned back and roared. Then its head snapped down and it threw itself forwards.

The girl stood no chance.

But at the last possible moment, she thrust her hands into the wolf's face, and hurled herself to the floor. She fell towards me, and I managed to catch her – knowing that in a few seconds we would both be dead.

Except that the wolf suddenly wasn't interested in us. It was rearing up, front paws tearing at its own face as it staggered back down the hall. I could see the doll's head lodged in its jaws. The wolf finally tore it free and the ragged head fell to the floor close to where the girl and I were cowering.

The wolf collapsed to its knees, then toppled forwards. It was convulsing, shivering, claws tearing desperately at the floor became hands beating at the floor. Human finger nails breaking as Britta convulsed one final time, and was still. A young woman lying dead across the narrow hallway of a tiny flat.

A few strands of dry, brown straw were clinging to her lifeless lips. The same straw that the doll had been stuffed with – I could see it spilling out of the neck of the doll's head close beside me.

And I knew it wasn't actually straw or grass or horsehair at all. It was dried wolfstain from Krejikistan.

'Vrolak,' the girl said quietly, and hugged me tight.

* * * *

The blood on her pyjamas was from a shallow cut on her side. It wasn't much more than a scratch. Certainly nothing in itself to worry about. I'd got away with a bruised neck and scratches down my chest, which I'd not even noticed.

Like the girl's wound, my injuries were minor. Normally, I'd not have worried at all. Bit of TCP and a plaster and away you go. By now, a couple of weeks later, it should all be healed and forgotten. Should be.

So there you have it. That's our story. That's why we came here. I just couldn't think of anyone else we could go to. And now you know where I found your name and credentials.

I'm afraid she doesn't understand very much yet. But we're getting there. I've got her into a local school and she's having extra English lessons of course. I've even persuaded the Home Office she can stay, which is harder than fighting off a werewolf any day.

But that's the thing about werewolves isn't it? Whether you call them werewolves or vrolaks or whatever. We can feel it, in our blood. Getting stronger all the time.

So tell me, Professor Stemper – how long can we keep it caged up and contained inside us?

How long have we got?

The Tides of Avalon
Jennifer Williams

The king looked down at his nephew, broken in the mud. Just before the end his eyes had turned red, just as the old wretch said they would, and there were coarse tufts of black hair on the backs of his hands, but he'd managed to kill the boy before it went too far; his breastplate was caved in, his chest a bloody ruin. Distantly Arthur could feel his own life's blood leaving through the wound in his side, but he wasn't going to spend too long thinking about that.

"This is an end to it, then?"

Percival dragged his eyes up from the churned mud and the bodies lying there. The boy's face was white with shock and his eyes glittered wetly with the overcast light. It was a face Arthur had seen many times, often on young men come too early to the battlefield.

"That is what he said, sire." Now the boy was looking at the gash in Arthur's side. "Sire, we must get you to…"

"Tell me exactly what he said, Percival. I would hear it now."

His squire shook his head as though to clear it.

"He said that Mordred was their last hope, sire, and that with him went all their plans for the kingdom. The line will die out now, left to become an echo of a thing, a memory in the hearts of men. They will be nothing but stray dogs, fighting over scraps." Percival cleared his throat. "That's what he said."

Arthur nodded and pressed his fingers to the wound in his side. The pain was tremendous, but somehow he welcomed it. To their right the river ran red and grey, rushing the souls of men onwards to their end. Ravens began to circle overhead. *This is what it all comes down to? A dead boy at my feet and the stink of my own guts, already festering?* Arthur hefted his sword from where it rested in the mud. *By all the gods, I can smell my own shit.*

"I hope it means something, Percival. Here, fetch my horse and get her ready. I'll be riding straight to the old forest."

Percival's eyes widened with panic. He made to put a hand on Arthur's arm and then thought better of it.

"You can't! I mean, my lord, we must take you to the surgeons and have them help you. There is a woodling woman there and they say she communes with the fey, and there is nothing she cannot heal…"

"Percival, my horse."

The squire shook his head and Arthur saw with wonder that the boy – a boy who had just lived through his first real battle and had killed his first men – was about to cry. It made him feel old.

"You'll never make it to the old forest, sire, not with that wound and travelling a-horse."

"Listen to your King, Percival." Arthur laid a hand on the boy's shoulder and squeezed. His wound burned and stabbed, but he ignored it. "Do as I ask."

"But if you should die on your journey…"

"I will not die on the way to the forest, Percival. At least not until I reach the lake." Arthur smiled bitterly. "Merlin has one last task for me, and while that promise goes unfulfilled he won't let me die. The bastard."

* * * *

He travelled alone. And wasn't he glad of that.

It would not do for his men to see him, pale-faced and sweating, his grip on the reins turning his knuckles white. The wound he'd bound up as best he could, trying not to look too closely at how the flesh had been raggedly parted. It was a struggle to sit upright on his horse, each step along the forest path a knife in his side. But slump he would not, because he was Arthur, and he was ever a stubborn man.

On all sides the trees crowded out the sky, all of them huge and black with time. This was one of the oldest places, a dark scar on his kingdom that most men considered haunted, populated only by ghosts and mad men. Arthur could hear the shrill calls of birds all around and the stealthy tread of other, larger creatures. Now and then he would hear the lonely bark of a she-fox, screeching for her mate.

My kingdom. She will carry on without me just as these trees have, and who will even know my name?

His fingers brushed the hilt of his sword and he took some reassurance from its weight against his leg. It would be difficult to give up.

"Arthur, you're looking well!"

A slim patch of shadow between the trees folded in on itself and became a tall, gaunt man with a tangled grey beard. He wore rags and furs, and there were bones and gems twisted into his wild hair. His green eyes were impossibly bright in the gloom.

"Merlin Demon-Born. I was starting to think you weren't coming."

Except that wasn't true. The old man's fishy stink was all over this forest.

"And miss this?" Merlin walked daintily between the snarls of holly bushes until he could place his dirty fingers on Arthur's mount. The horse snorted. "The great King on his final quest, bravely battling his final foe… death." His eyes narrowed shrewdly. "The wound is bad, yes?"

Arthur ignored him.

"Mordred is dead."

Merlin nodded, just as though he already knew; which Arthur supposed was entirely possible. The old man began to walk on down the path and the horse followed.

"Good," he said eventually. "Let that be an end to it."

They moved through the forest in silence. Beyond the canopy of dark trees the sun began to set. The shadows grew fat and bled into one another, and the sounds of the forest began to change as the animals who lived under the moon's light crawled out from their hiding places. Arthur shivered and flexed his fingers; they were starting to go numb.

"How much further?"

Merlin glanced up in surprise, as though he'd forgotten the king riding just behind him. In this light his face was long and strange and barely looked human at all.

"We will come to the lake in the dawn's light." His thin lips split into a grin. "Are you discomfited?"

Arthur grunted. The cloth covering his wound was brown and stiff with old blood, but every time he shifted in his saddle he felt another warm surge as his body rushed to betray him.

"I've bled greatly for your war against the dog-men, Merlin. A kingly corpse will do you no good at all." The old wizard laughed, a dry rattle like shingle on a beach.

"There is enough left in you, sire, more than enough. You are a very singular man, as I believe I have told you in the past. Who else could ride straight from a battle, mortally wounded, and still be sat upright on his horse? None, I tell you, but Arthur. King Arthur – the king of now, and the king of centuries as yet undreamed of. I've told you that, yes?"

Arthur grimaced, but his heart swelled at the words, as it always had.

"You have mentioned it."

"That is why it could only be you. One day, when your kingdom is ready, when it needs..."

There was a throaty roar just off to their right and the trees and bushes were torn aside. Arthur's horse reared, eyes rolling madly, as a huge, shaggy figure charged at them. It was a bear, jaws slathered with drool, its throat raw and pink. There was only madness in its eyes.

"Get back!"

Arthur pressed his thighs to the sides of his horse to save from being thrown into the dirt and drew Excalibur from its scabbard. Merlin appeared to have heeded his warning so well he'd melted back into the shadows, as there was no sign of the old man. The bear roared again, standing up on its back legs and raking its claws through the air. Arthur wrenched on the reins, causing the horse to dance backwards in a flurry of mud, and brought his blade whistling down towards the animal's head. He caught it across one side of its thick muzzle and carved away half its face – Excalibur was as fearsomely sharp as ever – and now the bear was a screaming vision of raw meat, a single black eye glaring out of that red ruin like a pebble.

But the creature wasn't dead. It roared again and lunged for the horse's throat. Arthur had time to see its teeth pierce horseflesh before he felt the horse buckle underneath him. He let go of the reins and took Excalibur in both hands, holding the blade above his head before stabbing downwards, and this time it was a killing blow. The point of the sword took the bear just above its right ear and it fell to the ground in a heap.

"Blasted creature!"

His horse fell forward onto its front legs and Arthur had to scramble off to keep from being trapped underneath. Blood gushed in a tide onto the forest floor, bear blood and horse blood together, and Arthur was covered from head to foot in both.

"I thought all the bears were gone, even from the heart of the old forest." Merlin appeared from between the trees again, speaking in the same tone of voice he might use to comment on the weather. "A walker out of time, this one."

"I'm glad you found it edifying." Arthur pressed his hand to his side, grimacing. "I've lost my bloody horse."

"I suspect this is no ordinary bear, sire."

As Merlin spoke, the filthy black fur on the animal's hide began to writhe and tremble. There was a rough tearing sound and the skin along the belly split open, releasing a cascade of ropey intestines followed by hundreds of pale, wriggling snakes.

"What…?"

Arthur took a hurried step backwards while Merlin drew a long, thin stick from within his sleeve and poked at one of the snakes, spearing it neatly on the end. He held it up to show Arthur while the other serpents wriggled and hissed in the undergrowth.

"You see the markings?"

The snake's white scales were daubed here and there with scarlet drops, forming a pattern Arthur did not recognise.

"I see them, although what they are..."

"They depict the Moon's true name, sire. This was no ordinary bear, but a demonstration of power." Merlin snorted. "A desperate move from a failing people."

"You mean the dog-men were responsible?"

Merlin nodded.

"They live, as we do, at the whim of the Moon, although in a slightly different sense. It doesn't matter; they cannot stop what I have put in motion." He paused and scanned the trees. "You can do nothing, hear me? Nothing!"

The forest had only silence in answer.

"You said it was over," said Arthur. The last of the snakes wriggled past his boot. He stamped it into the mud. "Mordred was the last, you said."

Merlin flapped a bony hand at him as though he were a fly.

"It is inconsequential. Come on, we've a way to go on foot yet."

* * * *

They walked for the rest of the night in near silence, with only the occasional grunt of pain from Arthur and the strange calls of night birds in the darkness above them. Merlin waited until the king was stumbling half-blind before pulling a shimmering globe of light from within his sleeve, and then they saw the forest revealed in soft ghost-light.

For Arthur it was a time of pain that seemed to stretch out forever. The agony in his side, that terrible internal tearing, blossomed into a hot wave that enflamed every inch of his skin. The forest was cold and damp but he was ablaze, a man of fire and gritted teeth walking endlessly, endlessly through the trees.

I should not have kept this promise, he thought – when he could think, when the pain didn't fog his thoughts completely – I should have died on the battlefield. A hero's death. They would have written songs about it. Instead I will shuffle to my end, with the stink of this forest in my nose and the company of a wizened devil.

But he kept going, because he was the king, and he was ever a stubborn man.

When the first pink light of dawn began to stain the sky overhead Arthur at first took it to be an illusion – there were bright stars in front of his eyes now, bursting and vanishing like sparks from a fire – until he realised that in the distance the ground was glittering with the same rose light. He rubbed a hand across his eyes.

"We are here," said Merlin. He pointed with the stick. "The lake."

Of course it was the lake. Within moments the trees to either side had thinned out and they found themselves on the shoreline of a lake so wide the other side was little more than a thick line of darkness. The dawn sky, violet now and streaked with ragged scraps of cloud, was reflected perfectly in the water.

A great mirror, thought Arthur.

All at once, the strength finally drained from his legs and he stumbled, falling to his knees in the tall reeds. Immediately Merlin was at his side, dragging him back to his feet with surprisingly strong arms.

"Not yet, sire. Not yet. Time to rest soon, but we must get you into the waters."

"Tell me again," said Arthur. He allowed himself to be half dragged towards the shore, wondering at how a skinny wretch like Merlin could manage it. "What will happen? Afterwards."

"Of course my lord, of course." They splashed to the edge of the lake and Arthur felt freezing water flow over the tops of his boots. "You will travel far from here to a place called, let us say, Avalon, and there they will heal you and give you to sleep. Arthur, the greatest and wisest of all kings, will sleep for many years, for centuries, until the kingdom is once more in need of you. Then you will wake and return."

They walked until the water was up to their waists. The cold of it seemed to ease the pain of his wound slightly and Arthur found some of the fog lifting from his vision. There was a stirring in the water out further into the centre of the lake, causing little waves to lap against his stomach.

"The sword, sire. Remember?"

Arthur drew Excalibur and a narrow shape broke the water in front of them.

"The Lady," said Arthur. His grip on the sword tightened a little.

The Lady of the Lake walked towards them. Her head was bald and sharp-boned, her skin greenish-white. Eyes that were more like a cat's than a woman's flickered back and forth between the king and the wizard, and she opened a wide mouth lined with teeth like fish hooks. She wore nothing but a covering of warty scales.

"You are as beautiful as ever, my lady." Arthur sketched an awkward bow.

She hissed at this remark, and held out her hand expectantly. The fingers were webbed.

"Must I really?" Arthur glanced at Merlin. "A returning king should have his sword."

Merlin's thin face was unmoved.

"It is what was promised."

Reluctantly, Arthur held the sword out, blade first, and the lady of the lake snatched it out of his hands. Its wickedly sharp edge didn't seem to worry her.

"There. It has been a good sword." Arthur frowned as the Lady examined it briefly and then dropped it beneath the waters. There was a silvery flash, and it was gone.

"Plenty of swords in your future, Arthur, don't pout. Now, we must prepare you for your journey."

Merlin gestured to the Lady, whose yellow eyes brightened with sudden interest. She reached below the water and when her hands came up again she carried a soft white globe, no bigger than an apple. It shone with faint pearlescent light.

"And what's that?"

"Just a way to bind your wound for the journey, sire. Now, try not to move."

Merlin's strong arms were around his shoulders again, so tight it was almost difficult to breath, and the Lady shot forward eagerly, lips curling back from her teeth in a mockery of a smile. She pulled back the ragged remains of Arthur's hauberk to reveal the wound.

"What are you... ?"

She thrust the white globe at his side and pushed, tearing the wound anew and causing a fresh gush of blood to darken the lake. Arthur screamed, but Merlin's grip was merciless.

"Do not take on so, my lord! This is the way it must be. You are the only one who could carry this burden for us."

Arthur thrashed as the Lady forced the globe into his wound, pushing it until the sides closed around it and only a sliver of white could be seen. She retreated and Arthur sagged, nearly passing out with the pain.

"Why?" He coughed up a wad of blood. "What are you doing?"

"Just the start of your healing, sire, that's all." Merlin smoothed his fingers across Arthur's brow, pushing away the loose strands of hair as tenderly as a mother with her child. "You will take this with you, and go where we cannot." The wizard's voice hardened and Arthur suspected he was no longer talking to anyone visible. "The dog-men will fall before us, yes, and the tides will rise. The tides will rise."

The Lady of the Lake hissed again.

"Here is your vessel, my lord." Merlin pulled Arthur upright in time to see a slim boat slide into view. It was made of a pale wood that was alien to Arthur, and there were strange sigils carved into its side. There were no oars and no sails.

"This is how I am to travel to Avalon?"

In answer Merlin and the Lady of the Lake took hold of him and lifted him bodily into the boat. Arthur lay on the bottom and looked up at the sky. The clouds were yellow.

"Go now, Arthur Pendragon, the King of the now and the shall be. Take our precious cargo with you, for we are too old to travel."

Shifting in the boat, Arthur turned to see Merlin and the Lady of the Lake looking down on him from either side. Their faces were deeply shadowed, but for the first time he noticed how alike they were. Had Merlin always had such sharp cheekbones? They almost seemed to poke through his thin, greenish skin. And his mouth… had it always been that wide?

There was a shudder and a jerk, and the little boat began to speed away from them, apparently moving of its own accord. Arthur felt a soft thrumming from below, as though a thousand tiny fingers were prodding him along. The faces of Merlin and the Lady were lost to him, but he heard his wizard's voice, cracked and inhuman.

"The tide will rise!"

* * * *

The boat travelled in silence.

Arthur lay on his back and looked up at the sky. The wound in his side was still an agony, and the white globe forced in there by the Lady's hard fingers had only made it worse, but that all felt very distant now, as though it were happening to someone else.

And in a way, it was, reflected Arthur. Soon he would be at Avalon and they would heal him anew, and he would wait there for this distant point in the future that Merlin had always spoken of when he'd rise again. He thought briefly of her, the woman with the shining white skin, and he did feel a moment of sorrow, quickly clouded with anger. I'll leave them all behind, he thought, and they will regret all the betrayals and the doubt.

The sky turned from pale blue to bright azure to indigo, and then huge purple clouds crowded over to shield him from the stars. Night came, but the burning of his wound kept him warm, and the sun rose again, passing over him like a comet. Again and again he watched the sky flicker through all its colours, until he could no longer tell what time of day it was or even how long he'd been travelling. He slept, on and off, and dreamed dark dreams of dog-men in the woods, tracking him by the blood that poured endlessly from his stomach, and of a woman as pale as the moon with scarlet writing on her tongue.

"Will it not end?" he said to the open sky when he woke. "I must either die, or be saved. Unless this is all one of Merlin's illusions."

The first sign that the journey was over came in the form of birdsong. Arthur lifted his head to see where the music came from and saw a cluster of shining spires, white as bone, reaching up into the sky. It was a city unlike any he'd seen; so bright it was hard to look at. From where he crouched he could see that the boat was sailing up a narrow river-way and to either side were broad walkways, carved from flawless marble. He could see figures in the distance too, now approaching at a run.

"I am here." Arthur shifted forward in the boat, trying to rise, but the wound was swollen now, pushing out his belly like a woman with child, and it was all he could do to stay upright. One of the figures on the walkway reached the boat and took hold of it, pulling it to the river's edge.

"I am Arthur, your king. I have been sent here to…"

Arthur faltered as he took in the face of his rescuer. Mottled green skin shimmered with scales, and eyes that were much too wide for a human face blinked wetly. She opened her mouth and it was like a door swinging open when the latch is broken. Inside there were teeth like jagged glass, row after row of them.

"We know why you have been sent." The voice was guttural and harsh. "You come bearing their children."

"At last!" Another inhuman face appeared. Arthur tried to shift his body to the other side, away from them, but together they reached out with wet, fibrous claws and dragged him back. Arthur saw his flesh parting where they touched him and blood began to fill the bottom of the small boat.

"You don't understand, I've been sent by Merlin. You are to heal me and I will live here, until it is time for me to rule again."

The strange figures weren't listening. They dragged him from the boat so that he lay, sprawled and gasping like a fish, on the hard marble floor.

"You? It is not you who will rule, warm bag of meat." The creature who had first spotted him grinned again. "You've bought our children safely home, as was promised, and once more we will thrive."

"Your children? I don't…"

"The tide will rise again," said the figure to his left, and all at once there was a surge of horrendous pain in Arthur's guts. He screamed…

…and something inside him answered.

"We go below," said the green woman.

Distantly, Arthur became aware of a great shaking beneath him, and the spires of silvery marble seemed to tremble.

"What's happening?"

"You've brought us hope, Arthur Pendragon. You meat-sacks, the dog-men, the fey, all of you will drown." The green woman bent over him and rested her hands on his swollen stomach. "The tide will rise and you will drown."

And all around him the city that may or may not have been Avalon sank below the waves.

Flaming Sword
Richard Dinnick

"You did this?"

Her face was taught and strained. Her usually pristine white shirt was stained with sweat and the features of her face were pulsing with the strobing red light that accompanied the military klaxon. This was Evelyn Green – Evie to her friends. She was squatting down behind a desk, hiding from anything that might be looking in through the small window inset in the door.

"I didn't say that," said Ade. He was slumped against the wall, clutching his knees to his chest. "I said the project I was working on has got out of control."

"That's a fucking understatement!" Evie looked away in disgust. "You know, I'm just a sailor. We carry guns; we face an enemy and fight. We don't hide in the shadows and hit out at people blindly."

"Evie, I thought we were friends. This isn't my fault!" he shouted.

"So run it past me one more time, Adrian."

Ade grimaced. She hadn't called him that since they'd first met over a year ago. "Look," he said. "You know the work we do here. You know I'm not some evil scientist…"

He broke off. Was that true? Wasn't this at least madness if not actually evil? He frowned. If only they could get out of there. His eyes flicked to the window that now had reinforced steel shutters clamped firmly in place. Beyond was the island, the outside world. These things felt a long way away now.

* * * *

Of course, the island was perfect as a naval base. It was big, secluded, surrounded by water and – since 1973 – joined to the mainland by a manmade causeway. This allowed for vehicle access from the mainland. Restricted, of course. But it certainly made Adrian Newman's commute a bit easier. He lived a little way up the coast, just south of Perth in Coogee and it took him just under an hour to reach HMAS Sterling once he'd stopped for coffee.

Only, that morning he hadn't stopped because he'd been running late. He'd driven the little Hyundai as fast as he dared and finally got to the turning off Point Peron Road that would take him across the causeway. But first he had to clear security. It was a routine that Adrian liked because of one thing: Evie.

Evelyn Green was a Chief Petty Officer in the Royal Australian Navy. To Adrian she was also a seriously hot brunette. She wore a tight, white uniform that accentuated her curves and the strain on her shirt made Adrian wonder what her breasts would be like without it. He thought about this a lot. In fact, that was why he'd been late that morning.

He brought the car to a stop at the square checkpoint and produced his civilian pass. Another Naval rating checked under the Hyundai while Evie leant in through the window and gave him a flash of her startling smile.

That was not the expression she wore now. Now she was angry. Disappointed. Scared.

And she had every right to be all those things, Ade thought.

Being one of the senior NCOs charged with base security, Evie could go pretty much anywhere on the island but her usual post was in the small office at the entrance to Adrian's building due to the nature of his work.

Adrian sped past the military airport and into the main complex of the base. Having parked the little green car in his usual spot, Adrian made his way to his desk in the small building on the periphery of the northeastern section. A board on the exterior wall declared "NATO/ANZUS ITA programme. Strictly no public admittance. Visitors report to Room 101."

The glass doors slid aside silently to allow Adrian in and he fished his pass from his pocket to present at the turnstile, under the watchful eye of an armed sailor. Ade stepped through the metal detector and moved away when it failed to make any sound. He never carried anything metal from the car and made sure his belt was plastic. It would only slow him down every day.

Adrian pressed on down the hall and, once again having to use his pass, into the changing room. Here he quickly donned sterile clothing and passed through yet another door into the lab.

The room was about the size of a tennis court and divided unequally in two. The smaller portion was visible through a bulletproof safety glass window that ran the length of the partition wall. This was known as the "fish tank" and within were half a dozen young code jockeys who looked like they hadn't slept in days – probably because they hadn't.

Adrian waved and received a couple of nods from those not plugged into the localised version of iTunes. There was no WiFi in the building and no other devices

– MP3 player, phone, or tablet – were allowed into or out of the facility. Only one room had a hardwired WAN connection to the internet and that was the "apple room", so named because it contained only one battered iMac; the old fashioned gumdrop shape G3 with a cathode ray screen and red plastic housing.

It was also the most secure room in the building. All the IT experts and coders could access any other room and use any device they found there. But no one was allowed in unless some kind of emergency protocol was in force. Adrian doubted he'd ever go inside. No one had since he'd arrived a year ago. He guessed that's why they used an ancient Mac and not a brand new one.

The reason for this lockdown on internet access was simple. What the letters ITA on the board outside stood for was: Information Technology Assault. Adrian was junior team leader on a project designed to build computer viruses that had military offensive capabilities. A Trojan that could detonate a PC or change it some way. Basically anything that can turn a laptop, desktop or tablet into a killing machine.

Adrian's particular project was polymorphic viruses. He loved them because they were, to all intents and purposes, alive. They could mutate themselves to avoid detection creating replicas that were impossible to identify as hostile by even the most up-to-date, state-of-the-art, whizz-bang security software. But he was not actually an IT guy. He was a geneticist.

Or an evil scientist. Depended on your point of view, he supposed.

For fourteen months Adrian had been working on a polymorphic computer virus that could mutate to such an extent that it could be passed to humans. He'd given this abhorent new virus a codename – Knowhow.

This was such a dangerous proposition that those involved manipulated robotic devices that altered DNA, in a sub-basement below the building while the code jockeys manipulated code from the fishtank. The results were then tested on an array of devices hooked up to rats and monkeys, also housed in the sub-basement.

That morning, Adrian's team was in what he considered to be an unnecessary HR meeting so he slid into his chair and booted up his machine, impatiently going straight for the overnight test results.

What he saw made him catch his breath.

At 02.10 sample code/DNA splice reference HGTR had caused its Non-Human Primate host (a Rhesus monkey) to enter what appeared to be a hyperactive mental state. Ade quickly switched to the CCTV footage and watched as the NHP started bounding around its cage, highly agitated. It was 02.13.

Two minutes later, the Rhesus monkey became very still, only its arms twitching sporadically. Ade put the playback on 2x speed until, seven minutes later, with no warning, the monkey's head exploded. Ade jumped back, but he had been unable to take his eyes form the screen. Then he hit the play button again to bring the footage back to normal time. There was little blood anywhere, and a small cloud of something hung over the collapsed body, becoming thinner as it bloomed out.

He checked the current time on the computer clock. It was 09.03. Seven hours had passed. Ade frowned. The monkeys were checked at 3am. He hit the fast-forward. As he sped through the intervening 4 minutes, the other monkeys in the room began to exhibit similar symptoms. But their heads did not burst like puffballs. Instead, they began to thrash at their cages and by the time a white-coated lab assistant entered at 03.00, the remaining five monkeys had smashed their way out of their cages.

As soon as the door opened, the monkeys attacked. Ade recognised the lab assistant. It was Craig. Although his face was difficult to see because the monkeys had attacked him, biting and ripping at his clothes and flesh.

Ade, reached blindly for the radio beside his terminal. Why hadn't the automated General Operations Directive quarantined the room?

* * * *

"You didn't know what you were doing, did you?" Evie shouted.

It was like a slap in the face and brought Ade back to the here and now. Then he realised just how loudly Evie had screamed at him. He waved his hands to quieten her, afraid of what was outside. But it was too late.

A face appeared at the small window in the door. Once it had belonged to Kimmy; once it had been human. Not anymore. The flesh was slick and silvery, almost like a fish. But it was the eyes most of all that caused a deep-rooted revulsion. Kimmy's eyes now had no pupils. Or so it seemed. Perhaps that had shrunk to dots. Ade didn't know.

He grabbed Evie and pulled her to the floor. The brunette realised she had brought the infected person to them. Across the room Sam started to cry and David tried to comfort her. Her sobs were almost inaudible, silenced by fear. They had found her and David in the canteen after the building had gone into lock down.

This was all down to the General Operations Directive that ran the building. It was a security system. Everything automated. Nothing happened unless the system said so. Doors didn't open, machines and lights wouldn't operate. It was state-of-the-art. It had to be to contain what they were planning to build – had built, Ade reminded himself.

"We've got this far," whispered Ade to Evie. "We just need to get to the exit."

"Or get to a radio," Evie added. Hers was missing…

* * * *

Evelyn had accompanied Ade down to the animal rooms when he'd radioed her. They took HazMat clothing and respirators from a sealed locker and entered the sub-basement. Right outside the elevator, they'd found Danni. She was just standing there, shaking. There was no way they could get to the Rhesus monkeys, but Ade had seen what had happened to Craig. His head had turned mushroom cloud, too.

"So is it airborne?" Evie had asked, her voice muffled by the respirator.

"None of the other monkeys have died, so it seems the virus has a different use for some hosts," Ade replied. He was trying to stay calm, to keep to the scientific analysis.

With Danni standing not five feet from him it was difficult. Plus his eyeholes were steaming up so he had to keep moving his head to see through the clear patches.

"Steady your breathing and the glass won't fog," Evie said. She stepped forward. "Danni? It's Evie. Evie Green. You OK?"

Danni hadn't moved at first, but then she'd turned and they had seen the effects of Knowhow on humans for the first time: the silvery complexion, spreading from a scratch in her face, the hyper-dilated pupils – they had made Danni look like an unfinished cartoon.

Evie had unholstered her side arm and levelled it at Danni. "Stay where you are," she said, her voice giving the merest crack on the last word.

Then all hell had broken loose. Another figure had appeared from the left and slammed Evie to the floor, scrabbling at her hood and mask. The gun had gone off, missing Danni and hitting a strip light in the ceiling. Then the gun had gone spiralling across the floor to Ade's feet and Danni had sprung at him, teeth bared and hands outstretched.

Ade had ducked to pick up the gun and shot at Danni. He'd never fired a handgun before and he had to loose off the whole clip of nine rounds to bring the infected woman down. He'd kept pulling the trigger. Click, click,

click. And still she hadn't died. She'd been moaning and twitching on the floor. Ade had dropped the gun and turned to his friend. Even unarmed, Evelyn had done better than him.

He wouldn't forget the sight. Evie had been squatting on the chest of what had once been a man, smashing her chunky radio into his face again and again, turning it into an unrecognisable pulp. Ade had managed to steady Evie's hands and pull her away from the dead man. They stumbled into the lift once more and had ridden up a floor, Ade ripping the respirator from his face so he could be sick in the corner.

As soon as the lift doors had opened, Evie had strode out, smashing the palm of her hand into the HazMat alarm. Straight away a klaxon had started sounding and red lights in the ceiling had begun to flash. The calm, authoritative voice of the General Operations Directive had come over the Tannoy system:

"This building has been declared a biological unsafe area. Please remain where you are. All exterior doors and windows will now be sealed."

"We need a G-O-D access terminal," Evie had said. "We need to contact SERP."

"The system will do that," Ade had replied, wiping his mouth on the hazard suit. "As soon as the alarm goes off the Serious Environmental Recue Protocol is called in."

Evie had simply nodded. "The elevators won't work anymore, but we've got to cover the stairs. Stop anyone else getting up here."

* * * *

They never got to cover the stairs. Before they could get there, they met a newly infected sailor. Thinking far more quickly than Ade, Evie had pulled him into a janitor's closet and smoothly closed the door.

"The virus is spreading!" hissed Evie, looking at Ade for answers.

Ade swallowed and did the best he could. "The only mercy is that it seems to be infecting patient zero differently."

"Mercy?" The word was spat out like a curse. "What do you mean?"

"As far as I can tell, Knowhow causes the initially infected subject of each species – patient zero – to explode and send out what I guess are spores of some kind.

"Lovely."

"The subsequent cases spread the virus by touch or saliva. Hence the biting and scratching."

When the infected sailor had passed, Evie opened the door and ushered Ade across the corridor into the canteen. Here, Sam, a secretary from central admin, was hiding by a cold drinks dispenser. She almost brained Evie with a can of Diet Coke, but David had stopped her.

The Kitchen was fitted with a General Operations Directive terminal, allowing Evie to ask some more questions. The system confirmed that the SERP Intelligence team had arrived and the building had been cordoned off. Ade had commented that the SERP: Int team would assume that everyone was infected unless they heard otherwise and that the whole building would be incinerated after two hours.

That's when Evie's interrogation of Ade had begun.

* * * *

Now, they had less than an hour until the building would be burnt and a Knowhow victim was staring at them through the door.

"Sam!" Evie called quietly. "Knives. In the Kitchen. Get me one."

But Sam didn't move. She was now sitting in a pool of her own urine and seemed almost catatonic. David was just stroking her hair.

"Great!" Evie said through clenched teeth.

"I'll go," Ade said and slipped away, passing under the small window in the door so the infected couldn't see him and round by the Coke machine into the kitchen. As quietly as he could, Ade started opening draws and cupboards, soon locating a selection of lethal looking cooking knives in one of the metallic drawers. He picked out two: one for Evie and one for him.

Suddenly, two hands snatched at his face, but Ade managed to duck down, jamming one of the knives into the infected's leg as he went. The sailor fell back, emitting an unearthly screech. Ade ran back to the canteen as the door burst off its hinges and Kimmy entered, lips curled back revealing what looked like razors for teeth.

Evie calmly took the remaining knife from Ade and flew at Kimmy, ramming the knife into her lower stomach and twisting it up into where her organs were. The silvery-skinned girl stumbled back, clutching her guts as the lower intestines started to ooze from her wound.

"Come on!" Evie called and Ade helped David get Sam up. Then they half-stumbled, half-ran down the corridor to the stairwell. Another Knowhow-infected ITA worker saw them and gave chase. Evie plucked a fire extinguisher from its wall housing and jerked it back into the oncoming infected's face. His head snapped back with a nasty cracking sound and Evie pressed on, kicking the door open and racing up the stairs.

"There's a security post on the third floor. We charge the radios there sometimes."

They managed to make it to the glass panelled room without encountering any further infected. Here a bank of spare radios stood and Evie grabbed one of them, tuning into the emergency frequency.

"This is ITA security. We have uninfected in the building. I say again: uninfected in the building. Please advise. Over."

The radio crackled with static for a nerve-wrenching second and then a calm, male voice came over the air. "This is SERP: Int, ITA. We read you. How many survivors do you have? Over."

Evie quickly relayed the situation and asked for evacuation.

"Negative, ITA," came the response. "General Operations Directive has the building in lockdown. We cannot connect to that system. You need to establish contact via apple room. Then we can hack the system using a Flaming Sword command. Over."

Ade looked at Evie across the table. "We can't do that," he said. "What if the virus gets out?"

Evie spoke into the radio, "Copy, SERP: Int. Give us a minute. Over."

She looked up at Ade. "I am getting out of here. I am not becoming one of them." She jerked her thumb over her right shoulder. "You can stay here if you want. You probably deserve to. But not me."

"I vote we go," said David, who had his arm around a totally silent Sam. "She needs medical attention. Now."

Ade ignored him. "Evie, please! We can try anything else, but not the apple room. Can't we blow up a door or a window or something?"

"You know that's not going to work," Evie straightened up and pressed the transmit button on the radio. "ITA to SERP: Int. We're going for the apple room. Over."

"Copy that, ITA. Good luck. We'll be waiting. Out."

Evie started walking away from the radio but Ade held her wrist. She turned "Don't touch me!" she whispered venomously and snatched her arm back. "If you're coming, stay close."

"The Knowhow virus. What if it gets out?"

"Don't you think SERP: Int will have figured that out? They'll have firewalls or anti-virus software in place. Whatever the hell you IT warriors use."

"I'm a geneticist," said Ade quietly.

But Evie wasn't listening. She was opening a weapons locker and taking two handguns from it. She kept both for herself and made for the stairs. Ade just followed close behind, with David and Sam bringing up the rear.

As soon as Evie pushed open the door to the stairwell, there was an infected there. He looked different. His eyes had become tinged with silver and the veins that were visible on his face and forearms stood proud of the skin, tinged with a metallic sheen. He reached out to grab Evie round the neck and the Chief Petty Officer had to unload her clip into the man.

He stumbled back but managed to make a final lunge and caught Sam's dress, pulling her towards him. David tried to pull her back, but the infected was too strong. He clutched the girl to him before a bullet took him in the head and he somersaulted backwards over the handrail, plunging to the basement level five floors down and taking Sam with him.

Ade just watched, uncertain of what to do. David screamed.

"We've got to keep going!" Evie took Ade's wrist and led him up the next flight of steps. David looked at the crumpled and bloodied body of Sam for a moment and then followed mutely.

All the time the endless klaxon and flashing lights filled the stairwell as it did the entire building. It served to numb the rising sense of hopelessness Ade felt.

On the fifth floor, Evie squatted down beside the door onto the corridor and opened it a fraction to reconnoitre the situation. She let the door close again gently.

"Well?" Ade wanted to have a look for himself.

Evie just shook her head. "Most of the ITA are out there," she said. "It's as if they know this is our only way out."

She slumped against the wall, deflated. "We need a plan." Evie turned to Ade. "I'm sorry if I've been a bitch. But I need you now otherwise we're all going to die here – or become like them."

Ade nodded.

Evie continued "So what I need is your best thinking on what might distract these fuckers. Or anything they might react badly to – other than a bullet."

"Radiation, I suppose," Ade said. "Um, anaesthetic?"

"What about something they would like? Something to draw them away from the apple room; something to give us a clean run?"

"Us," said David quietly. "They only seem interested in infecting others."

"Propagation is the primary purpose of any living thing and a virus is no different," Ade said.

Evie sighed. "So the only way to get them out of the way is if one of us goes out there, shouts 'hi, come and bite me' and runs off?"

Ade nodded.

"This is not what I joined the Navy for," Evie said.

"I'll go," said David. He suddenly looked up and there was fire in his eyes. "I'm fast. Give me the gun and I'll draw them off. This level's got a circular corridor around the central room. You can get to the apple room and I'll catch up."

They all knew this was bullshit. Evie nodded. "OK." She handed the Browning Hi-Power 9 mm auto to David.

He nodded back, opened the door and ran out, shouting and screaming like a banshee. Evie and Ade watched through the crack in the door as the infected all raced towards David and he took off down the corridor.

Evie immediately yanked open the door and started running too, heading for the apple room. If the apple room itself was the castle then the central room was the outer bailey. She and Ade reached the door almost simultaneously. Evie had her pass ready and pressed it against the small metal plate beside the door.

Nothing happened.

"What the fuck?" Evie shouted. Her pass got her in anywhere.

"Access to the apple room is not advised at this time," said the calm voice of the General Operations Directive. "Please confirm entry by representing your pass."

Evie slammed the plastic card against the metal plate once more and the door clicked open. She slipped inside and Ade followed. Then a gunshot made him turn.

"Wait!" The shriek came from David as he barrelled down to the corridor, a crowd of the infected in his wake. He was firing back at his pursuers without looking. Ade could see he was actually going to make it. He smiled.

Then David's head exploded.

Not with the puffball-like dryness of the monkey or Craig. This was like a balloon of blood. Ade's blood ran cold as he saw that one of the infected also had a handgun and had shot David. This was not something he was expecting. He thought that the infected were animalistic, had no reasoning or problem-solving abilities.

The first bullet hit the door above his head, ricocheting with sparks and deafening Ade in his right ear. But he heard Evie.

"Get inside. Close the door!"

Ade ducked into the central room and saw Evie standing at the inner door to the apple room, holding it open. Like the fish tank, its walls were embedded with glass panels so anyone in the central chamber could see what was going on in the apple room.

Ade tripped forward and fell into Evie's arms and she dragged him across the threshold, sealing the door with her pass and collapsing to the floor.

"They've got guns," Ade said between deep breaths.

"Who gives a shit?" Evie stood up and went over to the red iMac. She pressed the small button on the front of the machine. It whirred into life and with the signature sing-song tone, the screen lit up.

Ade had been so focussed on the machine he had not noticed the line of people that was forming outside the apple room. When he did he felt a last spark of hope die.

"We're trapped," he said.

"Uh-uh," Evie said. "Look up."

Ade raised his eyes and saw a metal hatch in the ceiling.

"Our escape," said Evie. "We just do what SERP: Int told us and they can hack the system, unlock the hatch and send a helicopter to pick us up."

Then Ade saw the infected sailor with the handgun. He took aim at the glass and fired. Ade threw himself to the floor, but Evie just laughed. "Dumbass," she said. "It's bullet-proof."

Ade stood up and looked into the pupil-less eyes of the sailor, his face was like a smooth metal mask. There were no lines, no pores. It was a freakish facsimile of humanity. As the sailor lowered his gun, the others infected with the Knowhow virus all thronged to the windows, pressing their horrific faces against the glass, leering in at the two survivors.

Evie was ignoring them. She was leafing through a small folder of plastic-sealed pages, tapping one-fingered at the keyboard or using the white mouse to click on an icon or command. After a few moments, she sat back.

"We're connected," she said.

Everything became still and silent for just a few moments. Then the calm voice of the General Operations Directive sounded over the Tannoy. "SERP: Int failure. Flaming Sword initiated."

Through the glass panel, Ade watched as the metal shutters that had been obscuring the external windows began to rise. All the doors in the building opened including the one leading into the apple room. The infected moved forwards now like wolves, circling Ade and Evie.

Then the Mac's screen went blank and a small back bomb icon appeared in the centre along with the two words. Fatal error.

COVENANTS
Simon Bestwick

"So," said Esther, putting down her pint. "How are you doing?" I opened my mouth to answer. "And don't say 'fine'."

I closed my mouth again, clinked the ice cubes in my whisky. "I cry a lot," I admitted at last. "When I'm on my own. Comes and goes. Other times, just – numb. Listless. It's like a virus. You just have to let it run its course."

"Have you been out at all since the funeral?"

"Just the shops." Outside, dead leaves blew in the November wind. We were in the Knott, an old haunt of ours; it's a pub in Manchester that offers good whisky, good real ale and excellent pub food. Sheila had always liked the place.

Esther nodded again. "What would help? Would anything?"

"Having Sheila back." I sighed. Esther tapped a steel-toed Doc Marten boot on the tiled floor. "Sorry. I dunno. Get away for a bit, maybe. Fresh air. Keep occupied."

"OK. That's a start. Any idea where?"

"I don't know," I said. But then I did. "Barmouth."

She raised an eyebrow. "Sure there wouldn't be too many memories?"

"Maybe just enough. Besides, she'll be there wherever I go."

Esther covered my hand with hers. "If there's anything I can do…"

"Fancy a few days at the seaside?"

"I've got some leave owing," she mused. "They've been on at me to take it."

"Well, then." All of a sudden, I liked the idea; it was the most enthusiasm I'd felt since Sheila's death. "I'll get it booked when I get home. Get down there tomorrow if I can."

"Hang on. Might not be able to get time off straightaway."

"That's OK. I can go down on my own. Join me when you can."

She bit her lip. "If you're sure. Call me if things get bad. Even if it's stupid o'clock in the morning."

I'd known Esther about four years before I met Sheila, and spent the first three trying to make her renounce spinsterhood in my favour. Once I'd finally accepted that wasn't happening, she'd become one of my closest friends. Sheila's, too.

"Don't worry about me. I'll keep myself occupied." I smiled. "Might look for the Ark of the Covenant while I'm there."

"What?"

*

Barmouth's a small town on the coast of North Wales. My dad grew up there; when I was little, we used to spend weekends or half term holidays there with my gran. After she died, I still paid the occasional visit; later, I brought Sheila too.

It's perched on the edge of the Mawddach Estuary, which opens out into Barmouth Bay (opening out in turn into the Cardigan Bay, which opens out into the Irish Sea) and boasts one of the British coast's few Blue Flag beaches. Behind it is the hill range Dinas Oleu- the Fortress of Light- and more hills rolling inland into the Snowdonia National Park. So there's a fairly steady tourist trade, which keeps the seafront guesthouses along Marine Parade in a fairly secure line of business. The Endeavour, where Sheila and I had stayed years before, was still open; it had always been a good place to stay, but I decided there'd be a few too many memories than I'd be happy with there; besides which, it only offered double or family rooms.

I explained my situation to the couple that ran it; they recommended the Belle Vue, a few doors down from them, which catered mostly to singles. It being November, there was no problem booking a room at short notice.

It was a four-hour journey from Manchester by train; once I'd unpacked the sun was sinking over the bay. I went out onto the beach and strolled along it till I reached the stepped concrete jetty that stuck out across the mouth of the estuary. When I'd been a boy, the beach had been more or less flat, with wooden groynes to help keep the sand in place; I'd caught blennies and shrimps for fishing bait in the pools around them. Now the groynes were almost completely buried by migrating sand and high dunes topped with marram grass split the beach in half lengthways. The lower steps of the jetty were buried too, and most of the stone promenade connecting it to the seafront. The seafront promenade itself was also choked with the drifting sand. In season they used JCBs to clear it away, but at this time of year it was suffered to build up.

By the time I'd walked from the jetty to the Quay, it was nearly full dark. I pottered over to the Last Inn, a quayside pub that served decent food, then walked back through the Old Town and over the railway crossing to Marine Parade. The town was silent. A couple of times I looked back, thinking someone was behind me, but never saw anything but dust and leaves and litter, blown by the wind.

*

I'd decided to keep to a strict schedule while I was up here, getting up early to take full advantage of the day; this time of year it'd be dark by five p.m. My alarm bleeped me awake at six a.m; I showered and dressed, then went for a morning run when it got light around seven. By eight I was rolling into the Belle Vue's breakfast room. I'd decided to skip lunch during my stay, taking advantage of the full English breakfast the hotel offered in the morning and refuelling with a substantial evening meal.

For the rest of the morning I pottered around the town; finally, though, my gaze turned to Dinas Oleu. It was a fine clear late autumn day, the air crisp without being cold, the perfect day for a climb. I got up and headed towards the mountain; the only thing I hadn't yet decided was whether or not I'd go looking for the Ark.

*

I was heading for Panorama, the most southerly of the hills, overlooking the Mawddach and giving you, as the name implies, a pretty spectacular view in all directions. It made for a substantial walk.

There were several narrow cave-like passageways that burrowed into the hillside. I stopped outside one in particular for about a minute, then carried on.

The last, increasingly steep leg of the climb led through thick woodland carpeted with yellow, gold and russet leaves. Finally the woods thinned out and a few minutes later I reached the top of the hill, slumping onto the rocks there and enjoying the rest, the clean air and the quiet.

Which made it inevitable, of course, that my mobile would choose that moment to ring. I was tempted to kill the call till I saw who it was. "Hi, Esther."

"Joe. How are you?"

"Top of the world, ma."

"Up one of your hills?"

"Yup."

"Well, I'll be joining you tomorrow, you'll be glad to hear. Managed to convince my manager."

"Excellent."

"I'll text you when I've got the exact train time. You're sure you're alright?"

"Fine." Or I had been, till she'd called and reminded me.

"Have you gone to find... you know?"

"Not yet. Haven't decided." That had been true, till I said it. By the time Esther ended the call, I knew my choice was made.

*

A narrow road runs from near the Panorama summit back down to the town – it's quick, though very steep, and after the long trek I was tempted to take it. But I'd made my decision now and wanted to act on it before my mind could change, so I picked my weary way back across the hills, till I reached the 'cave' I'd stopped outside before.

In fact it wasn't a cave, but one of several old manganese mines bored into Dinas Oleu in the nineteenth century. It was sunk into the hillside, and to reach the entrance I had to get through both the gorse and bracken that grew about it and the muddy ground where the water ran out of it. At the entrance I peered through a screen of overhanging roots and drooping brittle fronds into the dark; from beyond came a sound of dripping water.

No time like the present. It was almost three o'clock and the day had begun its slow, relentless dimming. I ducked my head and stepped inside.

*

"Don't worry," I'd told Esther, back in the Knott. "I've not gone religious."

"What, then?"

"When Sheila and I moved in together, we basically said we'd give it a year, and get married if we were still happy at the end of it. We were, so we went to Barmouth to celebrate. And Sheila came up with this idea of us each writing a letter to the other. Like a love letter, saying how we felt, but also making promises. To be faithful, honest, all that. To mark the occasion, you know? Show our commitment."

"That's quite sweet."

"But – this was the funny bit – neither of us would read the other's letter. We'd put them in envelopes, and then put them in a box, and bury the box somewhere in Barmouth, where it wouldn't be found. So that, in a hundred years, or whenever, someone might dig it up and see how committed we were to each other."

Esther laughed. "Actually, that's lovely."

"So that's why she called it the Ark of the Covenant. And we had to promise neither of us would dig it up, or else."

"But now you're planning to?"

I sighed. "I don't know. I like her idea, but I just miss her. I've still got old emails and stuff, but... I'd love to see her handwriting and see what she wrote. I don't know. I might just leave it. Might be better."

*

But I'd decided, in the end, it wasn't.

The tunnel stretched back about thirty feet before ending abruptly at a sheer stone face. The stone-strewn floor was ankle-deep in chill water, except for occasional rocks that broke the surface. I used them as stepping-stones, hands on the walls and ceiling for balance.

The tunnel got darker as I went. I tugged out my mobile and used the light from the screen for a torch. The tinkle of dripping water echoed in the tunnel; the water's surface danced with it. In the summer, I remembered, you'd find newts here.

I hunched low as I neared the back. What light came this far back reflected off the water and made rippling patterns on the ceiling. For a second it flickered, as if someone had moved across the mine entrance. I looked around, but there was no-one there. A withered fern was bobbing and nodding where someone – or something – had caught it. One of the sheep that grazed the slopes, maybe.

"Hello?" I called, but not too hard. It could have been another hiker, just passing by, not even knowing I was in here. But that fern was very close to the entrance. I shrugged, told myself it was just a sheep, and picked my way to the back of the mine.

As I've said, there was a lot of loose stone on the mine floor, and it was heaped up at the foot of the wall. By the look of it it hadn't been disturbed for a long time, which wasn't a big surprise; it wasn't easy getting this far back, and I felt cramped and uncomfortable already – not to mention very conscious of how much weight I'd gained since the last time I'd been in here.

I crouched down and started carefully moving the stones aside. Beetles and woodlice scuttled away as I did, no doubt bewailing the cataclysm to their quiet little polity. I muttered an apology to them but kept going, till at last an old, faded Marks and Spencer's carrier bag became visible.

"Shit," I said. My voice echoed sibilantly in the mine and I looked round. Still alone, the grey dimming afternoon light just visible through the entrance. Must be a sheep cropping the grass above the entrance, because that withered fern was still nodding. Although the sound I thought I heard sounded more like the scratching and scurrying of something smaller – rats, maybe.

Best to get this over with. I touched the plastic bag, feeling several layers of plastic underneath – then hard, unyielding metal. I cleared the rest of the debris away and prised the Ark out of the hole. The box, I remembered, had been an old biscuit tin, about a foot square and four or five inches deep. Pallid earthworms squirmed in the vacated hole.

I replaced the rocks as best I could, but I was in a hurry. A gull had cried out suddenly when I pulled the tin free – an odd, drawn out cry. It had startled me. I'd laugh about it when I was back down in the town, of course. I unzipped my rucksack, brushed the worst of the soil off the Ark and stowed it inside. I'd open it later.

I crept out of the tunnel and straightened up. The fern was still nodding, but there was no sign of a sheep; the wide slope above the entrance was completely empty. I peered up, wondering if I'd seen something move. Something must have, because a pebble came bouncing down the slope towards me, but there was only silence and stillness.

I pulled the rucksack on and started down the hill. The undergrowth, as I went, seemed to be alive with the scratching and scurrying of unseen things.

*

When I came down off Dinas, I was starving – a long climb will do that – so I made straight for the nearest restaurant. I was in no rush to open the Ark; the decision to dig it up in the first place had been a big enough step, and one I wasn't sure I didn't already regret. I'd broken my promise to Sheila as it stood, but not as badly as I would if I opened the box, or read the letter itself.

One large Chinese meal later, I felt much better, and walked back through the Old Town to the Quay. There's very little light pollution in Barmouth, and the clear sky above the town was full of stars. Across the estuary a speckle of tiny lights gleamed and more beyond it, at the headland down the coast. A light wind sang in the masts of the ships in the harbour, flapped at their sails.

I walked back along the seafront. The air was cool without being bitterly cold and I couldn't hear the wind; the only sound was the brittle hiss of waves breaking beyond the dunes. Streetlight drenched the concrete promenade and the drifts of sand piled thick against the sea wall, and layered on the ground a livid orange. The seafront looked abandoned, as if left deserted after some catastrophe, beautiful and eerie all at once.

After a couple of minutes I became aware of another noise – a sort of scuffing sound, like a dog digging at the sand. I turned, but there was nothing to see, just the empty seafront and the drifts of sand. It all looked a bit more desolate than I liked, and I wondered if Barmouth out of season really was the best place for me just now.

I walked a bit further, and then I heard it again. This time it was louder and faster, and went on longer. Not so much like a dog – maybe it was just its scuffing quality that'd made me think of that. Now I listened, it was more of a scratching, like dried twigs, but it made me think of something scuttling, like a crab or a spider, and it was still getting louder – because it was getting closer.

I spun round but nothing moved. There was someone else there, though, a man in a long, pale-coloured coat which fluttered around him in the light breeze. Or was it a cloak, or even a robe? It seemed to have a hood, anyway. He didn't move or speak, just stood there, watching me. Maybe it was just the distance that made his face look blurred, but I didn't think so.

I was almost opposite the Belle Vue, and started crossing over. As I did I heard the scratching, scuttling sound again, but when I looked there was nothing and no-one in sight; not even the man in the long, pale coat.

There'd been something familiar about the scratching sound, but it wasn't till I got back inside that I recognised it, or perhaps I hadn't let myself realise till I felt safer and less exposed. It had sounded like what I'd heard on the mountain, outside the mine.

Which brought me back to the weight in my rucksack, and a sudden burden of guilt. Any relationship is an act of faith, and carries with it the secret fear that you won't be equal to the enormity of your vows. Throughout mine and Sheila's time together, I'd kept the ones I'd made, both those publicly declared in the registry office and those other, more private ones now sealed in the Ark.

Was there perhaps, among all the grief at the loss, a kind of guilty relief that the test was over and I hadn't failed it? Then again, the test might not be over; the promise had been to leave the Ark in the ground forever, and I'd broken it.

I went upstairs, but slept fitfully. That's par for the course with me in a strange bed, at least for the first couple of nights. It didn't help that I kept feeling that I'd let Sheila down somehow; betrayed her trust, even, by breaking my word.

I had a brief, vivid dream of lying in the hotel bed in the small hours, listening to a twig-like scratching sound at the double-glazed bedroom window, and looking to see a pallid, shapeless face, framed by a gap in the curtains, with large, dark, irregular eyes and a larger shapeless mouth, peering through the second floor window.

*

Despite the poor night's sleep I was up at the usual hour next day when my alarm shrilled. I showered and dressed and went for my normal run.

Each day, I'd decided, I'd try to go a bit faster, achieve a bit more in the half an hour's running time. More laps, or – as today – running on the beach.

I managed several laps around the town and jogged onto the beach and over the dunes, as there were still a few seconds left to run. The stopwatch counted them off. I'd already been slowing, warming down, and now I let myself slow to a halt and bent, gripping my knees and breathing deep. The roar and thump of blood faded in my ears, and that was when I heard it again – that scuffing, scratching noise, coming from behind.

There was something unreal about it, the mix of dread and calm that washed through me in that moment. I took a deep breath and turned around.

About thirty feet away from me crouched a thin figure draped in a sheet that had been white but was now grimy and faded and tattered at the edges. It hung to the sand because the figure was squatting on its bony heels, its feet placed wide apart but drawn in close to its backside so that the knees were pointing sharply skyward. The sheet was rucked up around the thighs, but mercifully hung down between them. Something moved under the sheet's edge; two thin, bony hands crawled out, scuttling like crabs, and then were still.

The thing's legs were long and their thinness made them look longer still. They were like the legs of corpses in a concentration camp. Long feet, long toes, and long, yellow toenails that had curved like claws. The hands, the fingernails, were the same.

Where the sheet covered the head were three large dark irregular stains where some fluid had seeped through and then dried. They looked like huge inkblots and roughly corresponded to where you'd expect the eyes and mouth to be on a person. The sheet seemed to be sticking to the thing's face, if it still had one, in those places, as if glued there.

The pale hands scuttled further out from under the sheet, and further apart. The arms revealed as they did so were as long and emaciated as the legs; the figure's upper body tilted forward, but its legs stayed in exactly the same position.

When its body was tilted horizontally, its arms were bent at the elbows and its weight supported on its hands. It crouched on its four bent limbs, body suspended between them like a huge spider, and its head darted up and down and from side to side, twitching. Like a dog, sniffing for a scent. Then it stopped, went still, and its shrouded, sightless head swivelled smooth, like a mechanical part, till that face of blots and stains once more pointed directly at me. The eye-stains seemed to stare, the mouth-stain to scream.

I wanted to look away, seek witnesses or help, but I didn't dare take my eyes off it, because I knew it would move the second I did. Besides, there'd be no witnesses, not out on the beach at this hour. I'd wanted solitude; now I had it. The moment stretched out; the eyeless, faceless stare didn't waver. When it scuttled towards me, dismayingly fast, it was almost a relief. Before I turned and ran I had time to register that, as it went, its long curved nails scratched at the sand with a noise like brittle twigs.

I ran directly along the beach. I was behind the line of dunes and didn't dare try to scramble up them with that thing right behind; one slip and it'd be on me. Instead I went for the jetty, going as fast as I could, trying not to think of how fast he thing could move. The length of those limbs, the speed they'd worked at. I scrambled up the gentler incline to the jetty, but I was still floundering in the sand and I could hear those scratching, scrabbling nails in the sand, closing on me.

I heaved myself up the slope and onto the jetty's stone top, near the gap that led onto the half-buried promenade connecting it to the seafront. The wind picked up as I neared it; thin streams of windblown sand snaked around the corner, stinging. I looked back -

And nothing was there. The beach was empty.

The only sound was the wind, the hiss of sand, the sound of waves. No scratching, no scraping. I took a deep breath and started back towards the seafront.

*

I forced as much of the full English breakfast down me as I could, went to my room and opened the rucksack. There was the Ark, still wrapped in the Marks and Spencer's carrier, and several others under that to protect it. I hadn't unwrapped it, although I lifted it out now and put it on the dressing table.

I reached out to start unwrapping it once or twice, but couldn't. I wished I'd left it in the bag. I'd almost been able to convince myself by then that I hadn't seen the thing on the shore, that it'd been a dream or hallucination, but the Ark brought everything else back in a tumbling rush: the noises outside the mine, the ones that had followed me down the hill, the figure in the white cloak or robe the night before and the one on the beach this morning. I already wished I'd left the Ark on the mountain. I was tempted to go straight back up there to put it back, but I'd be on my own, with no-one to see what might happen. I was afraid; I knew it but also knew how little evidence I could produce for it.

Esther had sent a text; her train was due around four o'clock. A long time to kill, and there wouldn't be enough light to safely climb Dinas Oleu. I stuffed the Ark back inside the rucksack, then shoved it under the dressing table and went out.

I spent the morning pottering around Barmouth, browsing in second-hand bookshops and the big auctioneer's shop on Church Street, and enjoying a coffee at Davy Jones' Locker, the little stone-built café overlooking the Quay. Anything where there were people; anywhere I wasn't alone. Gulls cried out forlornly over the harbour and I winced, remembering the noise that had sounded when I'd uncovered the Ark. I finished my coffee and started towards the seafront. There were people on the beach now – a couple with a small child, a man throwing sticks for his dog – but I still shied away from going back there.

Eventually it was quarter to twelve, and I pottered through the town towards the station. Safety in numbers, I kept telling myself, safety in numbers.

*

"Joe." She kissed my cheek, frowned. "You look rough."

"Not slept well."

"Hmm." She sighed. "Come on. Let's drop my stuff off."

One thing about Esther is that she's a very methodical lady. She always goes packed for every eventuality and has to have everything in exactly the right place. There was only an hour of daylight left and she'd take well over that to unpack. So once she'd checked in, we took a stroll around the town.

We walked to the end of the jetty to watch the sunset, even though it brought me closer to the beach than I was comfortable with. I did my best to keep up the pretence that all was as well as could be expected for now. All the same, with Sheila gone Esther probably knew me best, so I doubted I was fooling her.

Back at the hotel, she shooed me out of her room so she could unpack. I couldn't face my room on my own – not even when I could hear Esther moving around directly above – but there was a common room in the guest house with a billiard table, a TV and a bar. I put the TV on and waited till at last she came down.

"Right. Where can we eat?"

I took her to the Last Inn, where she grumbled at the lack of vegetarian options and marvelled at the veggie-burger they served her. "It's like something out of the Eighties," she said, then leant back in her chair and studied me. "You don't look well, Joe."

"I've not –"

"Been sleeping well. Yes, you said. That's not all, though, is it? Come on."

I told her about the Ark, and how I was wishing that I hadn't taken it. "I'm going to go and put it back tomorrow."

"Maybe best. What else?"

"Nothing."

"Joe."

"OK." I told her about the sensation of being followed – the odd sounds, the figure on the seafront – though not about the apparition on the beach that morning. Speaking of it would make it real, somehow.

From the way she looked at me, I think she guessed I was still holding back, but she shrugged. "Doesn't sound like this was the best thing for you after all."

"Maybe being on my own wasn't the best thing. Might be better now you're here."

"We'll see." She was looking at me closely, still frowning. Then she sighed. "We'll see. Now, where's the dessert menu?"

*

After the meal, we stayed at the pub for a few more drinks, and the conversation shifted to other, lighter topics before we walked back. I led us through the town, wanting to keep clear of the seafront, though it was so still and silent it didn't really make much difference. We said goodnight, and I stripped to my underwear and crawled into bed.

With strange beds, the third night's usually the charm, and despite everything I was soon asleep. Esther's presence helped, that and the resolution to return the Ark to its resting place unopened. I just wished I'd plucked the courage up to do it today; my fears of going up the hill alone seemed small now.

Then I was awake. I wasn't sure of the time; it was still dark, except the dull glow of streetlight strained into the room's murk through the curtains. Early hours of the morning, perhaps. Whatever the time, I was awake, and fully so. I lay on my side in the bed, blinking, listening. I didn't know what had woken me, but I knew something had. Something very specific. After a few seconds, I heard it again; what sounded like twigs scratching at the glass of my bedroom window.

The scratching continued, but its quality changed. Before it had sounded like a blind, undirected groping and fumbling, now it was a steady sound of picking and scratching, and it sounded focused, as if the owner of those thin, clawlike hands had found a single point on which to concentrate its efforts. I wanted to go back to sleep. I wanted to get up, turn the lights on and throw back the curtains. I wanted to run out of the room. I did none of these things, but just lay there listening as the sounds got faster.

Then there was a new sound, a faint metallic clinking, then a dull clunk and a squeak of hinges. I told myself that you couldn't open a double-glazed window from the outside. I was still trying to convince myself of it as the cold draught entered the room from outside, and grew stronger as the window widened.

I had to get up; I had to do something. But I couldn't move, not even when the scratching sound resumed, now inside the room, to be joined by the slither of some heavy object dragging itself in through the window. Not even when the streetlight spilled more fully into the room through the parted curtains and threw the silhouette of a shrouded torso and long, emaciated arms across the floor.

The light flickered as it fell; a crash and tinkle as the vase of artificial flowers was knocked off the windowsill. Something landed with a muffled thump on the floor; claw-like nails scraping at the carpet.

I sat up in bed in time to see the blind swaddled head swivel towards me and show its face of stains. Able to move at last, I heaved the bedclothes at it and lunged for the door.

I have a habit of locking the room doors in guesthouses; luckily I hadn't in this case. I yanked it wide and ran down the stairs.

At the foot of the first flight, I looked up. The bedroom door swung closed behind me. The Ark, I realised, was still in my rucksack. If that was what it wanted, maybe it would take it and go away. Maybe it would end there and -

From the room came scuttling, then a scratching noise. When bony, yellow-clawed fingers slid round the edge of the door and pushed it wide, I knew it wasn't the Ark it wanted.

I ran. I didn't have much idea where I was going, just away from that thing. I didn't look back, but I could hear its scrabbling footsteps as it raced after me. This time, I knew it wasn't going to be gone when I turned around. I might have shouted, cried out; I don't remember. I was making enough noise as I ran.

All I could think of was getting outside. Outpace it somehow. Flight after flight of stairs. The front porch; yanking the door open. Bitter night air. Sprinting across the road; hard tarmac under bare feet. Cold. Night wind. Across the promenade. Panic. Run. Get away.

Down onto the beach. Feet plunging into the clingy sand. Memories of old public information films about people leaving glass on the beach to break and set traps for unwary feet. Rusty tin cans too. I'd been paranoid about going barefoot on beaches for years after that. I ran up the dune ahead of, clutching handfuls of sand and marram grass. From behind came the scratching, the scuttling.

I made it down the side of the dune, saw moonlight gleam on the water only yards away. The tide was coming in. Nowhere left to run. Better to drown? I ran another couple of yards in the darkness before my bare foot went straight into a rock. The pain shocked through me and I let out a howl of pain as I flew forward.

Rolling in the sand, looking back. A hunched, spidery figure in silhouette at the top of the dune, then a scrabbling like a dog digging madly for a bone as it rushed down it. Trying to rise, to run again, but it was too late. The dirty, stinking sheet, stains for a face, bony hands and yellow nails. The long arms shot out, and it had me.

*

I don't really remember much after that. I was covered in scratches, shallow but bloody. How much damage could it have done me, if Esther hadn't got there? I honestly don't know.

Esther, yes. She hadn't felt tired, she explained to me later, so she'd been sat up reading when she'd heard the thunder of running feet directly above her. She'd called my name, just heard panicked footsteps barrelling past. She'd been getting up to investigate when she'd heard the front door bang, and gone to the window instead, in time to see me pelting across the road in my skivvies, and – yes – what was chasing after me. So at least I know it wasn't all just in my head, although the damage to the lock on the bedroom window went some way to proving that too.

Esther had run out after us. Because she was still fully dressed, she had her boots on; steel-toed Doc Martens, remember? When she got over the dune, I was on the ground with the thing crouched over me and clawing at my face and arms. Without thinking, she ran in and drove a kick into its side. It flew sideways, as if it weighed nothing, long limbs thrashing about, keening like a wounded gull.

Later that night, after she'd got me back to the hotel and cleaned me up, Esther said she thought it had power over me, perhaps, because of what I'd done; she was a different kettle of fish, of course. She ran and kicked at it again and again, not letting it rise. It rolled into the surf. She kept kicking, then stamping. When she stumbled backwards there was almost nothing left of it. Even the sheet had broken apart into unidentifiable rags. The surf hissed around the remains like acid; breaking them up, carrying them away.

*

The next morning we went up Dinas Oleu together. I was limping badly and still had a couple of scratches on my face, but I'd heal. Physically, at least. At least the Belle Vue's owners seemed to have no idea what had happened, though they'd looked askance at us the next morning when they saw my face.

Esther offered to put the Ark back, but I didn't let her. It had to be me. She kept watch outside the mine entrance instead, holding a stout walking stick she'd bought at the auctioneer's before setting out, just in case.

I crouched and picked my way back into the mine, found where the Ark had been easily enough and pressed it back into place before carefully piling the stones back over it. If it was disturbed again, it wouldn't be by me. I listened out for noises; I might have heard a gull cry or some faint movement, or maybe that was all I expected to hear.

"It wasn't her," Esther said when I came out. "I don't know what it was. Something you or her or the two of you made somehow, without meaning to. I don't know what, or how. But it wasn't her, Joe. It wasn't Sheila."

"I know," I said. "I know."

"It'll be alright now," she said. "It will."

I wondered which of us she was trying harder to convince.

She took my arm, and we slowly started back down.

The Second Coming
Wayne Simmons

Ali was cold.

Squatting naked in a damp basement would do that to a girl.

She checked the strength of the cuffs. Still tight. She remembered begging for them to be just a little looser, but Simon hadn't given in.

Why the hell do I let him do this to me?

Ali knew the answer to that, of course.

She'd been into the whole scene for five years or so – ever since her marriage had fallen apart. After ten years of feeling absolutely nothing for a soulless shell of a man, Ali needed to feel something.

And Simon made her feel a whole lot of something.

He touched her, scratched her, spanked her in all the right places. He made Ali feel all kinds of things, in all kinds of ways. And she liked it.

But she didn't like this.

Leaning back, Ali assessed her situation. Simon's place was a one-room wonder – a low rent basement apartment: kitchen in one corner, bed in the other. Ali was naked, cuffed to the old cooker, arms bent backwards, cold hard floor below her knees.

She couldn't loosen the cuffs. But maybe if she used all her strength she could somehow pull herself free from the ring she had been cuffed to.

She raised herself onto her feet, one leg at a time, then used her petite body as leverage to pull against the ring.

Pressing forward, she felt her arms strain behind her. The harsh metal of the cuffs was biting mercilessly. Fresh wounds were opening around the skin on her wrists. The joints in her arms were straining, the pain hard to bear.

After two futile attempts, Ali fell breathlessly to her knees again. The cuffs remained secured to the cooker ring.

Outside in the stairwell, Ali could hear a low moaning sound.

It wasn't the first time she'd heard it. This was the same sound that had disturbed them before. Ali had asked Simon to check it out. He'd been pissed off, reluctant to let anything spoil their game, but went all the same. Someone might be hurt, she'd told him. Simon had pulled a shirt on, found his shoes. Said he would check the stairwell, maybe call upstairs to make sure everything was all right.

But that was a couple of hours ago, maybe more.

Ali had given up calling out Simon's name, satisfied that this wasn't part of some new and innovative game he'd dreamed up.

The sound of shouting now. It was coming from upstairs. Maybe the next apartment.

Is that Simon's voice?

Then she heard crying, someone begging for mercy. Definitely Simon. But Ali had never heard him cry like that. He was her dom, for Christ's sake!

Another noise, like someone being choked.

And then nothing.

Ali waited.

Her heart started to thump, and dark thoughts clouded her mind.

Fuck. This is it.

There was someone in the apartment block. Some maniac or serial fucking killer, she knew it. They'd killed everyone else in the building. Killed Simon, and now they were coming for her.

Ali pulled uselessly at the cuffs, shaking her hands to and fro, banging them off the cooker ring, but it was no good.

She was trapped. Helpless.

On a normal visit here those were words that would excite her. Ali had played the willing slave in every sordid little fantasy Simon could dream up; she was always the prisoner, he was always her captor.

He would make her beg for mercy, reward her when she did what he asked, punish her when she didn't.

It had all been a game, his move, her move. Role play.

But the game was over and Ali was beginning to feel real fear.

Her eyes suddenly widened.

In the pale light, she noticed a pool of dark liquid seep in from under the door to the apartment.

The moaning noises returned, getting louder.

Struggling again to her feet, Ali tried to pull herself free, succeeding only in drawing more blood from her wrists as the hard edge of the cuffs bit further into her skin.

"Fuck!" she cried, then stared back towards the door.

The sounds were getting louder.

The dark liquid ebbed ever closer, pooling around her naked toes. It looked like blood. Smelled like something altogether more foul. Its stench filled the room, thick and acrid. She could almost taste it in her mouth.

Ali turned away. Tried to stop herself from throwing up.

She noticed the power switch for the cooker, had an idea.

Straining one last time, Ali clambered back onto her feet, her arms once again forced into an unnatural position. Leaning to one side, she turned her body as much as possible, stretching one foot towards the cooker power switch on the wall. She curled her toes, trying to block out the excruciating pain of the metal cuffs slicing deeper into her gashed wrists as they bore the entirety of her weight. Ali cried out, stretched further, managed to switch on the cooker with her big toe.

She fell back down.

The blood on the floor was everywhere now, cold and wet against the skin of her knees.

Tears were streaming down her cheeks, snot building up, unchecked, around her mouth and nose. Her heart was pounding, her head beginning to feel light.

This was hell. Ali was naked and helpless and these fucking cuffs were really killing her.

But she had to see this through. It was her only chance…

Ali twisted one shaking hand around the dial of the cooker ring, almost immediately feeling its warmth against her trapped hands. She waited, then pushed the edges of the cuffs against the glowing cooker ring, ignoring the pain as her torn wrists were scorched by the increasing heat.

A banging sound. It came from the door.

Turning, Ali watched the door crack against repeated force. Someone was trying to break into the apartment. Again they pounded. And again. Soon, the entire door was beaten off its hinges.

A tall shadow loomed over the doorway as the broken door fell away. Ali's eyes struggled to make out more, but it was too dark.

Crying, she pushed the cuffs harder against the heat. Her wrists felt raw, the high-powered cooker ring now glowing red, its energy charging through the metal handcuffs.

The shadow drew closer, forming in the light.

Ali felt every part of her body tense.

She screamed uncontrollably as, what appeared to be a decrepit and naked man, shuffled awkwardly into the apartment.

The figure cut a terrifying profile; its long hair and beard matted with the same gore gathering at Ali's feet. It was drenched in the stuff, mostly oozing from a thick crown of rotting wood woven around its head. Its face was barely recognisable; strips of torn and rotting flesh hanging together. A piece of skin slowly peeled from its cheek, dripping onto the floor.

Ali choked breathlessly as one gaunt hand suddenly pointed straight at her. More gore dripped from its palms, where gaping holes had formed. Each of its feet bore similar wounds

The creature stumbled clumsily in Ali's direction, its haggard face towering over her as she cowered by the cooker. Ali pulled frantically against the now red-hot cuffs, the heat brutally melting the flesh around her wrists, raw fear and adrenalin providing the anesthetic she needed to finally pull free.

With a cry of relief, Ali stood up, her arms becoming horizontal for the first time in over an hour.

But the creature was on her.

Ali acted on pure animal instinct, grabbing a nearby bread knife and burying it in the foul thing's chest.

The creature stumbled backwards.

Looking down at the new wound, it appeared confused… hurt. And then angry.

It lunged for Ali, curling its cold, clammy hands around her throat.

Lifted her with surprising ease and pushed her heavily up against the nearby wall, fixing her with its dead-eyed gaze.

Ali froze. The pressure around her throat suddenly reminded her of some of the things she liked to do with Simon.

But then a thousand other things rushed into her mind, things which Ali regretted, things which she was ashamed of. Her life flashed before her eyes, a mishmash of pain and grief. There was no love. She couldn't remember ever being happy.

But she didn't want to die. Not here. And not like this.

Tears broke from her eyes.

The creature seemed to notice, its head turning to one side as it watched her grieve. Allowing its grip to relax, the creature stepped back a little. Fixed its eyes on Ali, the cold, hard expression on its face seeming to soften.

The creature lifted a small mug from the nearby table, peeled some of the ragged flesh from its skin and dropped it in. It added some blood, before raising the mug to Ali's quivering lips.

With sudden and unexpected clarity it spoke: "Take… Eat… This is my body. Drink… This is my blood."

The vile contents were forced down Ali's throat, the putrid smell and taste making her gag repetitively.

Somehow, Ali managed to swallow. The hand around her throat loosened completely and Ali found herself tumbling to the ground.

The creature moved slowly away. Its rotting feet padded heavily on the kitchen floor as it stalked back through the doorway. Ali watched it disappear from view.

And then everything changed. With an unexpected jolt of lucidity, Ali suddenly understood. It felt like she'd just cum, a mind-blowing orgasm shuddering through her body, leaving her warm inside, feeling high. The world and its secrets became clear for the first time in her life.

Lying on the floor, her naked flesh stained with blood, Ali began to laugh and cry simultaneously. Relief and euphoria raced through her veins. It felt like she had been washed clean of all the things that had made her feel so wrong inside.

Everything that she had once valued in life now seemed ugly and repulsive.

And what had seemed monstrous was now her salvation…

Simon was gone, but Ali didn't care. She had a new master now, one that made her feel beautiful and pure. She had no doubt that He would show her new things, touch her in new ways, make her come in ways she had never known.

Even though her new master had left her, alone and broken on the floor, Ali felt no resentment.

In time He would return to her.

She listened to the sounds bleeding in from the still night air. Sounds of carnage. Of death and despair. Her dark Messiah continuing His work.

Ali smiled.

Knowing she was one of the blessed ones.

One of the chosen few.

The Lips of Every Sleeper
Alison Littlewood

The first thing Thomas heard when he awoke was the woodland, and he knew before he looked out of his window that it would be soft and dark and still; but he also knew that its stillness was an illusion born only of distance. The woodland was never still and never quiet. Whenever he had played there it was full of noises, glad noises; the shouts of his friends, the wind stirring leaf and branch, the sudden bright colour of birdsong, the rustle in the undergrowth that made him think of rabbits but which usually turned out to be a crow or some other bird foraging for whatever it found there.

He hadn't been in the woods in a long while, though, and never after dark. Still, he knew that something was different even before he slipped out of bed and pulled back the curtains. There was something wrong about the sound he could hear, which swelled as he slipped the catch and pushed open the window. It was too loud, to start with; he couldn't usually hear the woods at all when his window was closed. That, and there were voices in it.

They weren't happy voices like those of his friends, not calling or shouting. He looked towards the edge of the wood, opposite his back garden and across a small, scrubby field. It was formless and dark, as he had expected. It was as he had found it before, many times, save for the singing.

It rose again now in a soft swell, making Thomas think of branches lulled by the breeze, but it wasn't quite like that. He thought for a moment of the church that lay on the other side of the trees, of choirs singing perhaps, but it wasn't like that either; it was as if the wood itself had been given voice and the sound had carried to him on the cold air, something solemn and mournful and sad. It made Thomas think of things that were sad too, and he stood and listened for a while, though he wasn't really looking at the woodland any longer. That was when he heard something from the room next to his, the room that had once been his sister's.

He frowned. Lucy's room was empty; it was always empty now. He had trespassed there while she lived in it, but now she had gone, he kept out. Only his mother went in there sometimes; she went in and sat on the bed, her hands resting on the coverlet, staring at nothing.

Thomas knew this because he had seen her, had looked in through the open door and into her face, and he had frozen, only his heartbeat suddenly giving a painful stutter. But she hadn't seen him, although he had been in front of her face, and he had walked on and the moment had passed.

There was a soft thud, as of someone slipping out of bed and onto the carpet. Thomas caught his breath. He didn't move but he felt his bowels contract, as if his insides had been squeezed in a giant fist.

He didn't expect the sound to come again, but it did. Someone was walking across the carpet. They were walking towards the door, which led on to the hall, which led to Thomas's room. And then he remembered who was in the room, all at once, and he let out the long breath he hadn't known he'd been holding.

'Thomas?'

It was his grandma's voice; grandma who was staying with them, just for a while, to see if his mum needed any help.

Thomas didn't reply but his door opened anyway and she was there, small and thin in her nightdress, which was pale and went right down to her feet and up to her neck and ended in a little lace collar. Her hair was white and unbrushed, standing straight out in some places and flattened in others.

'I – I heard something,' Thomas muttered. 'Sorry, Gran. I'm going back to bed now.'

She didn't answer. Instead she crossed the room on her bare feet – Thomas hadn't seen them before, the pronounced joints, the white hairs that grew on each big toe – and then she stood beside him. Tom realised he was staring and looked away; but she hadn't noticed. Instead she was focused on the window, and he only understood that she was holding her breath, too, when it rattled out of her lungs.

She stretched out one wavering hand and pulled the window closed.

'Gran?'

'Shh. Back to bed with you, Tom.'

She was the only one who called him Tom. With his mum and dad he was always Thomas.

He turned and got into bed and pulled up the quilt. She kissed his forehead. Her lips were dry.

'What were they singing, Gran?'

She pursed up her lips. 'Something sad, my dear.'

'But – who is it?'

She looked at him then, but he couldn't make out her expression. 'You shouldn't listen to them.'

Tom fell silent and so did she. He realised he could still hear the voices, rising and falling through the glass. From his grandmother's face, he knew she could hear it too.

'Shh, now. It's only the dryads, Tom. They come out at night, when no one can see. They sing to mourn their fallen sisters.' She stopped abruptly, as if she'd just realised what she'd said. 'I said shush, Tom. Sleep tight.'

She turned back to the window before she left, pulling the curtains across the gap, hard, as if she could shut out the sound that drifted still through the panes of glass.

* * * *

'What's dryads, Grandma?' It was the first thing Thomas had thought of when he'd woken, still with the taint of sadness on his tongue, as if he could almost taste the music he'd heard in the night. The moment he'd spoken, he frowned; surely it couldn't have been real. The whole thing, waking in the night – perhaps he'd only dreamed it. But grandma looked up, her eyes sharp – not at Thomas, but at his mother – and he knew it had been real after all.

After a moment, when mum didn't say anything – she just kept stirring the eggs she was scrambling – grandma pushed her cup of tea across the table and shifted to the seat next to his. She spoke quietly, so that he had to lean in closer.

'Dryads is just one name for them,' she said. 'They're the spirits of the trees, Tom. They live inside the trees – but they *are* the trees too, if you see what I mean. Once, everything had a spirit that lived inside it. Lakes, rivers, mountains. Everyone knew it. Now no one believes any more.' She winked, so that Tom wasn't sure if she was serious.

'They're afraid of nothing but axe and fire. When the tree dies, they die. They pass out of this world and – well, there aren't any new dryads, any more. Not like in the old days. When all the *old* trees are gone – they'll have forgotten us and we'll have forgotten them.' Her eyes shone as she warmed to her theme.

'There are yew trees just beyond that wood. Maybe it's because of them the dryads come: there are no trees as old as a yew. Some of them are thousands of years old. They've seen things you'll never see, things that will never come again. They're sacred.'

Thomas frowned. He couldn't remember seeing a yew tree in the woods. But *beyond* it – yes, he knew there were yew trees beyond it; he knew exactly where they were to be found. They grew in the graveyard where his sister lay. He looked at grandma's face and saw she had thought of it too. She glanced at mum, who was staring down at the frying pan. The eggs were beginning to burn, coating the back of his throat with an acrid smell.

Grandma got up and went to help. That was why she was staying with them, after all: to help. Thomas stared down at his knife and fork. He didn't feel hungry any longer, and then a plate of thick, dry egg landed in front of him.

He remembered something else and he felt sick. He closed his eyes. He could see grandma standing in front of him, wearing her long white nightdress, her hair outlined in moonlight.

They come out at night, she had said, *when no one can see. They sing to mourn their fallen sisters.*

* * * *

It had been bright daylight when Ethan had first mentioned the tree-house. Thomas had been lying flat on his back, tired and a little sweaty, sucking on a blade of grass. Josh had a blade of grass too, but he was holding his in a funny way between his hands, and when he blew on it, it made a whistling noise that Thomas hadn't been able to replicate. It was something Josh did when he was bored.

Thomas was looking up into the branches, which swayed softly with some breeze that he couldn't feel, not down here. Perhaps that was why Ethan had thought of it: maybe he too had dreamed of flying up into the highest boughs of a tree and feeling that cooling breeze on his face.

'We could build it,' Ethan said. 'We can get some rope and tie branches together. We could make a ladder and a platform. And no one would know about it, only us. It'd be our clubhouse.'

Thomas grunted. Ethan was always coming up with ideas; it didn't mean they were going to happen. They rarely did. When he glanced over, though, he saw that Josh had pushed himself into a sitting position, his eyes fixed on Ethan. He pushed himself up too.

'It'd be great. We could have a password and everything.' He waved a hand around, indicating the clearing where they lay. 'There are loads of branches,' he said. 'Loads and loads. All we have to do is pick them up.'

And so they did. They gathered branches, the strong and the dry and the brittle, all together, and stacked them in a pile at the base of a well-grown ash tree. When they had done, Ethan stood back and looked up. 'There', he said. 'Where those two big branches stick out.' He looked at Thomas. 'We're going to need some rope,' he said.

Thomas ran back through the woodland, jumping over fallen logs and branches. The sun was higher and he was hot, but it didn't bother him. What did bother him was that he was the one who lived nearest the wood. When they got thirsty, Thomas had always been the one to fetch cans of coke. When they were hungry, he was the one who'd run back to ask for bags of crisps. And this time it was him who'd have to raid the family shed.

Raid, because his mum never would have agreed. She didn't like him climbing trees. He got the feeling she wouldn't have liked him playing in the woods at all, if it didn't keep him out of the way.

This time, as he approached the shed, he was surprised to see Lucy sitting in the garden, under the apple tree. She had a white cloth spread out across the ground and her dolls sitting in a circle. The sun fell through the branches, dappling her hair, lending it a golden shine. Beneath it, her skin was pale.

Thomas skidded to a halt, but it was too late; she had already seen him. Her eyes widened and he put his fingers to his lips.

To give her credit, Lucy didn't shout for mum; but she didn't leave him alone either. Thomas opened the shed door and saw the old tools and shelves of debris from gardening years gone by, and sensed her at his side. He didn't look at her. He was breathing in the sheddy scent of the insides of empty plant pots and stale grass clippings. There wasn't any rope. There was, however, a ball of thick green twine, which he snatched and stuffed as far as it would go into his pocket.

He turned to Lucy and forced a smile.

Her eyes were wide and blue. They narrowed as she frowned. 'I'm coming too,' she said.

Thomas sighed. 'No, you're not. If you try it I'll run. You can't keep up.'

'I'll *tell*.'

'See if I care.' Thomas knew that if he didn't seem to care, there would be no reason for her to tell. Sometimes it worked, sometimes it didn't. This time it seemed to work. She turned away and her gaze went back to her dolls.

Thomas didn't explain and he didn't say goodbye. He just turned and went past her, heading back towards the woods, the twine bulging from his pocket. He looked back only once, to see her watching after him over the gate. Her frown had deepened into a scowl. Thomas turned and carried on his way, relieved that at least she hadn't followed him.

* * * *

Nothing seemed to go right, even from the start. Ethan climbed up into the tree and stood there while the others passed the gathered wood up to him. Ethan balanced it across the branches, but they wouldn't seem to stay in position. Everything was the wrong shape, or too twisted, or slipped when he tried to lash it together. The twine, Thomas knew, was too thin. Ethan hadn't said so – not yet – but only because he didn't have to.

Another branch fell from the bundle and Ethan swore. The ball of twine landed on the ground, rolled, settled a short distance away. A moment later, Ethan leapt down and landed beside it. His t-shirt was blotched with damp stains, his face smudged with dirt. His arms were covered in scratches. He kicked at the twine. 'Useless,' he said.

Thomas felt like apologising, but he did not. *Always me*, he thought. *Always me to fetch everything. In a moment he'll ask me for a drink*.

But Ethan didn't ask for a drink: he didn't ask for anything. He simply fell to staring, his head cocked back, up at the tree. Eventually, he spoke.

'Do you know what would be more fun?' he said.

* * * *

And so Thomas made his way back through the trees, just the same as before except that he was feeling hotter and more tired, and when he reached the garden he couldn't see Lucy anywhere; there were only the dolls, sitting in their mute circle.

He paused this time, looking at the house. He didn't think anyone had seen, and that was important. This time, he couldn't afford to be seen.

The axe was leaning with the other tools in the corner of the shed. Thomas wrapped his hands around it, lifting it just an inch off the floor, feeling its weight.

'What are you doing?'

Thomas jumped, dropping the axe. The bang resounded against the wood.

Lucy was wide-eyed, just like before. Thomas stared at the thing she held: a miniature teacup. He couldn't seem to speak.

Lucy smiled. 'I'm coming with you,' she said.

* * * *

Ethan swung at the tree. It was Thomas's axe, but Ethan had taken it from him without a word, and Thomas had let him. He swung over and over like a mad thing, splinters flying from the trunk. The axe was old and a little blunt and it wasn't long before Ethan was sweating.

He paused, looking up at where those two thick branches emerged from the trunk, an odd look on his face, as if the tree was defying him somehow.

Lucy stood by and watched. She didn't say anything at all.

Thomas was thirsty, but he watched too, until the trunk had thinned, a wedge missing from it. It was the shape of a slice of pie.

'It's no good.' Ethan paused. 'This isn't any fun anyway.'

Thomas glanced at Lucy. She looked as if she was about to laugh. 'Here,' he said. 'Let me.'

He swung the axe, realising at once that it was harder than Ethan had made it look. It was heavy and difficult to aim and the shock of hitting the wood shivered down his arms. But he had taken the axe: it was *his* axe. He couldn't stop now.

He went on and on chopping at the tree until it let out a long pained moan. They shuffled back a few paces and stared at it. It seemed a long time before it began to fall.

Thomas had expected a loud crash that would make them laugh, but when it collapsed into the ground the noise was more like an elongated crackling sigh. It made him feel disappointed and a little sad.

They all stood there without saying anything. Thomas was surprised when Lucy spoke first.

'Why did you do that?' she said.

No one answered. Thomas could *feel* his answer, though, inside his head. They hadn't done it because they needed the wood or for the tree-house or for any good reason at all. *To hear the crash*, is what he thought but didn't say.

Lucy looked at him. And he realised she hadn't been about to laugh at them, after all: she was trying not to cry.

'I hate you,' she said, and she turned and began to run, alone, back through the woods.

* * * *

It's only the dryads, grandma had said. *They come out at night, when no one can see. They sing to mourn their fallen sisters.*

And then came the words that Thomas couldn't seem to get out of his mind:

They're afraid of nothing but axe and fire. When the tree dies, they die.

Sleep tight, now.

* * * *

Lucy had already been sick when they'd cut down the tree. It had been growing inside of her, though they hadn't known it until afterwards. Thomas had stopped going to the woods after that. He had wished himself there – many times, when the silence in the house descended like a thick, suffocating blanket – but to find his friends, enjoy their noise, didn't seem right somehow. It was as if he belonged in the silence.

Thomas looked at his mother's face and he knew it was in her too, the silence. Her face was thinner than it had ever been, and her hair was covered by a headscarf. They were in church. They hadn't visited his sister yet. Flowers were clutched in his mother's hand, as if they would be blessed somehow by the dry words emerging in a monotone from the old man in the pulpit.

Thomas knew that words didn't help. Words, indeed, could be the problem: *I hate you*, she'd said, and he couldn't seem to expel it from his mind, especially after she got sick and he did not. He could hear her saying it still, *I hate you*, and there was the look of her, nothing on her bones but skin, and the blankness in her eyes, and the *smell* of her.

Thomas swallowed hard and closed his eyes. When he did, it was better. He could hear the dryads again, the music of the trees. It was sad, but there were no words in it. Sometimes, it was better that way.

Grandma took Thomas's hand as they went to the grave, and he let her. He stood while his mother knelt and arranged the flowers and then grasped the sides of the cold stone, just sitting there with her head bowed. He felt a jerk on his hand and they walked away and turned and waited.

'She'll be all right, you'll see,' grandma said.

Thomas wasn't really listening. He wasn't looking at his grandma and he wasn't looking at his mother either. He was staring up, instead, into the great heavy branches of the tree his sister had been buried beneath: the ancient yew that stretched its boughs across her grave.

* * * *

That night, Thomas heard the singing again. This time, when he slipped out of bed, he only paused briefly to look out of his window. The line of trees was dark but seemed thicker somehow, as if they'd huddled more closely together during the night. Did they seem a little nearer too? He wasn't sure. He pushed his feet into his shoes and pulled his coat over his pyjamas and headed for the stairs.

The night was cooler than he had expected, and clearer too: when he looked up he could see stars powdering the sky, so far away and so cold, and he shivered. The music rose around him on the rustle of the trees and there were words in it after all, though he couldn't make them out, didn't know what they meant. He started towards the field, finding the path was still known to his feet though he hadn't trodden it in so long. And he looked up and saw the trees and caught his breath.

There was a line of figures at the wood's edge, palely dressed, tall and slender. They held hands as they sang their bitter song, and Thomas forced himself to take a step towards them and he saw their faces were pale too, no life left in them, only cold forms that didn't shiver, that didn't seem to feel the chill. One of them was smaller than the rest. She wore a thin white dress and it looked as if her feet were bare. Her hair was gold and her eyes held a blank shine.

I hate you, he thought. And then the shrieking began and he turned, his knees suddenly weak, and his mother was there, grabbing at his arms and shouting and soothing all at the same time, and Thomas started to cry.

I saw her, he kept trying to say. *I saw her*. But it didn't matter how he tried to make her understand: she didn't seem to hear his words at all.

Later, grandma put him back to bed. She tucked the covers in tight and stroked his hair and sighed.

'I *did* see her,' he said.

'Shh. You're upset, Tom. You shouldn't wander off like that.'

'But—'

'I know.' She paused, her dry old hand still resting on his forehead. Thomas wanted to shake it off, but there was a look on her face: something far away and musing, and he didn't want to spoil it.

'Maybe you did,' she said. 'You know, they used to say – *my* mother used to say – that the roots of trees could reach the lips of every sleeper. That maybe they knew things—' she broke off, roused herself. She turned to the door, as if she'd heard something on the landing. 'That's enough, Toms. Goodnight, now.'

* * * *

The next day the taxi came and when Thomas got up his grandma was already standing next to it, her suitcase packed by her side. He shook his head. She wasn't supposed to be going, hadn't said anything about it: why would she leave now? He threw his arms around her. 'You can't go,' he said. 'You need to tell me what you meant. About the trees. About the sleepers.'

He felt her hands in his hair, but when he looked up at her she glanced away.

'It's time for your gran to go back now,' his mother said. 'It's all been planned from the start.' There was something in her expression. She wouldn't meet Thomas's eyes either; she wouldn't even look at grandma.

'Say goodbye, now,' mum said.

'But—'

'Say goodbye.'

Thomas hurried after the car, waving. Grandma waved too – not her usual cheery wave but just once, over her shoulder, and then she turned away. The car disappeared around the corner. Thomas stared after it, then turned and pushed his way back into the house. He'd said he needed to know what she meant, but a part of him suspected he already knew. *Sleepers*, she'd said. That's what people said when they were trying to avoid what they really meant, wasn't it? When they really meant the person was dead.

The roots of trees could reach the lips of every sleeper.

Thomas threw himself down onto his bed. He didn't want to think about it, not any more: but all he could see in his mind's eye was the dark roots, pushing their way down through the earth, snaking between rock and stone until they reached a small white coffin. He wondered what sound they would make as they peeled back its lid.

* * * *

That night, Thomas sneaked out again. He crept carefully down the stairs so that they didn't creak and turned the key really carefully and pulled the door open slowly and carefully, so that when it stood wide the only sounds he could hear were his dad snoring upstairs and the rustling of the treetops. For a moment he felt poised between them, the safe indoor sounds and the strange outside ones, and then he made his choice and stepped out.

He frowned. There was no singing from the woods, not tonight, and when for a moment the breeze stilled, there was nothing: not even the sound of his own breath. He thought again of dark roots, a pale coffin, and he shivered.

He went first to the garden shed. The axe was there, where he'd left it that last time, leaning in the corner with the other tools. He almost felt it should bear some trace of its crime, but there was nothing; the blade didn't glow. The handle wasn't slippery with blood or sap. He hefted it in his hands and turned towards the woods. They were dark and quiet and still. He looked up; there was no moon. It was a long way through the trees, and he knew he'd have to do it in darkness.

He cut across the field, his feet remembering the track, and paused at the edge of the trees. There were more fallen branches than he remembered; the shadows were deeper. It wasn't until he'd stepped beneath them that he saw they were there after all, standing tall and straight amid the tall straight trunks of birch and ash and oak. They were women all, with immobile faces and dark eyes, and they were watching him.

Thomas swallowed. There was a blockage in his throat. The axe was heavy in his hands and slippery now with his sweat. The women looked back at him. They didn't sing and they didn't speak a word.

There was something wrong with their faces; Thomas could see that even from where he stood. Their skin was sallow and lifeless, blotched with what looked like mould, blighted with cancerous growths. Now that he was beneath the trees, he could smell a sour, rotten mulch.

He forced himself to step past them, gripping the axe tighter. They turned and watched as he passed by and he shuddered. He fixed his eyes on the ground, then forced himself to look; he couldn't bear the thought of brushing by a tree and finding instead that pale clammy skin, soft and mossy, its touch staining him perhaps, tainting him with its disease.

And then he remembered his sister, the small shape he thought he'd seen standing among them, and he let out a gasp, stifling it at once. He half-turned. But he hadn't seen her, not this time; he hadn't expected to. He didn't feel this was where he would find her, though he remembered the place; he was standing in the clearing where he'd once played, hoping his little sister would leave him alone; that she would be gone.

I hate you.

He blinked, looked up, and saw a woman with a fringe of tangled hair standing before him. He clutched the axe, holding it in front of him, and she drew aside. Now he couldn't see her any more. He bowed his head and went on, through the woods; went on until he could see what lay at the other side.

The churchyard was limned in silver, each gravestone casting its own black shadow. The moon had risen after all, touching everything with its glow; everything except the trees. They looked as if each one had been replaced with one a little taller, a little darker.

Thomas passed under the lychgate and wound his way around the path. He saw no one, and no one saw him.

He stood under the yew tree where his sister had been buried.

'I came,' he said. 'I want to talk to you.'

There was nothing but the shifting of branches in the breeze.

'You've seen my sister,' he said. 'I know it.' And he gripped the axe and hoisted it and swung it towards the tree. A thin branch gave and sprang back, wiry and strong.

'I'll do it,' he said. 'I don't care how long it takes.'

There was a sound behind him. It was a little like a laugh, a little like a sigh. He turned and a woman was standing on the path, and she had the moon on her skin and on her hair, and a slight smile playing on her lips, which were full and poisonous as berries. She was beautiful. Thomas had expected her to be old, and she *was* old, he could see that; but her skin was smooth and unblemished, though pale as a night in winter.

She didn't speak. She just looked at him. Thomas found himself wondering if he was supposed to look away, but it didn't seem to matter; it was as if he was looking into the black immensity of the sky, and it reflected back nothing but his own unimportance.

'Do you know her?' he asked. 'Do you know my sister?'

Slowly, she nodded.

'Can you hear her thoughts?

She closed her eyes, bowed her head once.

'Then please . . .'

She glanced towards her tree, then to the axe in his hand. 'We each lost a sister, Thomas.'

He caught his breath. After a moment, he set down the axe. 'I'm sorry,' he said.

She looked into his face. He felt she were searching each part of him, sifting through the layers of his being, reaching down into him like roots. Her eyes were dark, but a cold light shone inside them. 'I hear the dead, Thomas. I hear their sorrows and the slow turning of their thoughts. Things pass. Things pass and other things take their place.'

Thomas glanced up once more into the sky, the distant and impossible glimmer of stars. Her words were simple, but he could never really understand them; he knew that, when he looked into her eyes.

'You're not going to tell me,' he said, and his voice choked. He looked down at the headstone, its edges already starting to weather, the slow creep of ivy at its base. *I hate you.* His sister had passed on, as the woman had said, and this is all that remained, something cold and indifferent, no words left.

'I can tell you what she thought, Thomas.'

The woman's voice was so soft he doubted for a moment he'd heard her speak. He raised his head.

'I cannot say if you will like to hear it.'

Thomas's breath froze in his throat. He could see his sister's face, looking after him from her seat in the garden, surrounded by her dolls and her little cups. The tight, suspicious look. Then the triumph in her smile when she'd said: *I'm coming too.* The sorrowful question she'd asked in the woods when the tree fell: *Why did you do that?*

The way she'd scowl when he'd taken something that belonged to her. The wail when he pulled her hair. The screwed-up nose when he tripped her; the dismay when he ran from her, so fast he knew she'd never be able to keep up.

He let out a sob; he couldn't stop it.

'Do you really want to know, Thomas?' She reached out a hand towards him. 'If you will . . .'

He stared. Her lips *were* poison, he knew that now. He could see it dripping from her, dark and bitter and full of promise, like blood. She could show him things, he knew. He could know what his sister felt; he could ask her himself. All he need do was kiss those lips, and he would know everything. It was the reason he had come, to ask this woman – this *thing* – of the poisoned tree. He could already feel the cold, creeping into his joints, slowing his thoughts, making his limbs turn to stone.

Lucy, he thought. He could speak to her again. She could tell him the things she knew. She could tell him all of the things that, deep down, he knew already.

Lucy. Sometimes I hated you too. But I love you.

He shook his head.

The woman withdrew her hand and stepped back, into the shadow. When Thomas tried to make her out he saw only a tree: its twisted trunk, rough bark, sharp needles, ripe berries; and every bit of it laden with death.

Things pass, boy. Things pass and other things take their place.

He turned back towards his home. Had they missed him yet? He had a sudden stricken feeling that they must have. His father, saying little these days, sitting watching the television for hour after hour but really staring at some unspecified place somewhere above it. His mother, wrapped in her headscarf, not speaking the way she used to: not laughing.

He felt tears on his face. *The lips of every sleeper*, he thought. All this time he'd been reaching after his sister, and now he knew he'd been reaching after the wrong thing all the time. It wasn't the lips of the dead he needed to reach but those of the living.

He turned and began to run back towards the trees. When he passed under them, this time, there was no one there; he couldn't even sense them watching him as he ran through clearings and pushed his way beneath the branches. The pale figures had withdrawn into their cold, hollow homes. The wood was empty now, only the wind left to whisper between the glades.

He reached the edge of the trees and paused. Away across the field, he could see his home. Lights were shining in the windows and the door was open. There were two figures standing outside, and they were waiting for him.

ABOUT THE AUTHORS

Stephen Gallagher is the author of fourteen novels including *Valley of Lights, Down River, The Boat House,* and *Nightmare, With Angel*. His most recent is *The Bedlam Detective*, continuing the exploits of ex-Pinkerton man Sebastian Becker after *The Kingdom of Bones* (2007). TV work began with *Doctor Who* and includes miniseries adaptations of his novels *Chimera* and *Oktober*, and the British and American versions of *Eleventh Hour*. A Stoker and World Fantasy Award nominee, winner of British Fantasy and International Horror Guild Awards for his short fiction. More online at www.stephengallagher.com.

Scott Harrison is a novelist and scriptwriter who has written novels for TV and game tie-ins such as *Remember Me: The Pandora Archive* (Capcom), *Star Trek: Shadow of the Machine* (Simon & Schuster) and *Blake's 7: Archangel* (Big Finish). He has written plays for a number of audio ranges including *The Confessions of Dorian Gray* and *Blake's 7: The Liberator Chronicles*, while his comic book scripts and short stories have appeared in a variety of anthologies, most recently *Into The Woods: A Fairytale Anthology, Resurrection Engines* and *Faction Paradox: A*

Romance In Twelve Parts. His novels *History Zero* and *Cold Earth* will be the first two books in the new Alternate History / Steampunk novel range *Tales Of The Iron War*, published by Snowbooks in 2014. He regularly blogs at http://scottvharrison.blogspot.com/

Justin Richards is the Creative Consultant to the BBC Books' range of *Doctor Who* publications, and has written a fair number of *Doctor Who* books himself. He is also a well-known writer of children's fiction for all ages. The first book in Justin's science fiction series *The Never War* is published by Del Rey in November 2013.

Kaaron Warren has lived in Melbourne, Sydney, Canberra and Fiji, She's sold many short stories, three novels (the multi-award-winning *Slights*, *Walking the Tree* and *Mistification*) and four short story collections. Two of her collections have won the ACT Publishers' and Writers' Award for fiction, and her most recent collection, *Through Splintered Walls*, won a Canberra Critic's Circle Award for Fiction. Her stories have appeared in Australia, the US, the UK and elsewhere in Europe, and have been selected for both Ellen Datlow's and Paula Guran's Year's Best Anthologies. She was shortlisted for a Bram Stoker Award for "All You Can Do is Breathe", and is Special Guest at the Australian National Science Fiction Convention in Canberra 2013. You can find her at http://kaaronwarren.wordpress.com/ and she Tweets @KaaronWarren

Jennifer Williams is a fantasy writer from South East London with a love of history, animation and very large swords. She has had a small flurry of short stories appear in a number of places, and her debut fantasy novel *The Copper Promise* comes out from Headline in Spring 2014. When not frowning at notebooks in cafes or fiddling with maps of imaginary places, she can often be found gesticulating wildly at her games console or haunting bookshops. These days Jennifer lives in one of the more eventful parts of London with her partner and their cat. Find her at www.sennydreadful.co.uk

Alison Littlewood is a writer of dark fantasy and horror fiction. Her first two novels, *A Cold Season* and *Path of Needles* were published by Jo Fletcher Books. Her short stories have appeared in magazines including *Black Static*, *Crimewave* and *Not One Of Us*, as well as the British Fantasty Society's *Dark Horizons*. She also contributed to the charity anthology *Never Again* as well as *Resurrection*

Engines, *Midnight Lullabies* and *Festive Fear 2*. Visit her at www.alisonlittlewood.co.uk

Hailing from Lancashire, **Simon Bestwick** is the author of the horror novels *Tide of Souls* and *The Faceless*, the chapbook, *Angels of The Silences*, and the short story collections *A Hazy Shade of Winter* and *Pictures of The Dark*. As well as writing scripts for radio, his short fiction has appeared in various anthologies, including *Where the Heart is*, *Never Again* and *The End of The Line*. His novella, *The Narrows*, was shortlisted for the British Fantasy Award. Find him at simon-bestwick.blogspot.co.uk/

Gary McMahon is the author of a wide variety of horror novels, novellas and chapbooks, including the much celebrated *Concrete Grove* trilogy and the *Thomas Usher* books. His short fiction has been published in a variety of collections and anthologies including *Tales of the Weak and Wounded*, *The Mammoth Book of Best New Horror* and *The Year's Best Fantasy and Horror*, as well as the portmanteau audio anthology *Thirteen*. He can be found at www.garymcmahon.com.

Richard Dinnick has written novels, audio plays, short stories and comic strips for several well-known and much-loved TV franchises such as *Doctor Who, Sapphire & Steel* and *Stargate,* as well as *Moshi Monsters* and *Sherlock Holmes,* and his short stories have appeared in *Doctor Who: Short Trips – The Solar System, Bernice Summerfield: Present Danger, Encounters of Sherlock Holmes* and *Stargate Magazine.* He is currently a scriptwriter on the CBeebies TV show *Tree Fu Tom.* His website is www.richarddinnick.com

Born in Belfast, **Wayne Simmons** has written half a dozen novels in the horror genre that have been published in the UK, Austria, Germany, Spain, Turkey and North America. His latest novel, *Plastic Jesus,* was published by Salt Publishing. As well as novels, Wayne writes reviews and features for the online sites ZombieHamster and Lair of Filth, and co-produces the Scardiff Horror Expo. You can catch up with him at www.waynesimmons.org

Susan Murray is an Open University graduate and serial house renovator who lives in rural Cumbria. She writes fantasy and science fiction with occasional forays into other genres. Her short story *Flashpoint* was longlisted in the 2012 Bristol Short Story Prize. Susan can be found on Twitter as @pulpthorn.